MW01092612

Happy Hollow
518 Happy Hollow Rd Murrayville IL 62668
Sponsored by: Peace on the Prairie

Stormstruck!

John Macfarlane

Holiday House / New York

Library of Congress Cataloging-in-Publication Data
Macfarlane, John.
Stormstruck! / by John Macfarlane. —First edition.
pages cm
Summary: Believing his parents are going to euthanize Pogo,
a beloved yellow Labrador that had belonged to his deceased brother,
twelve-year-old Sam sets sail with the dog and gets caught
in a terrible storm along with Magnus, a hermit, and his pet tern,
Fuego, whom they meet on an island.
ISBN 978-0-8234-3394-0 (hardcover)
[1. Adventure and adventurers—Fiction. 2. Survival—Fiction.
3. Storms—Fiction. 4. Labrador retriever—Fiction. 5. Dogs—Fiction.
6. Islands of the Atlantic—Fiction. 7. Sea stories.] I. Title.
PZ7.1.M245Sto 2015
[Fic]—dc23

To Salty

N
W   E
S

Mainland
25 miles

Fog Island Sound

Fog Island Harbor

tide rips

rocks

FOG ISLAND

breakers

breakers

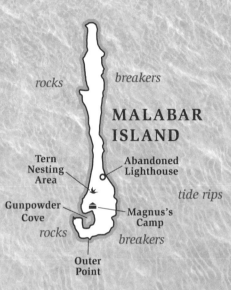

tide rips

tide rips

Wreck

rocks

breakers

tide rips

MALABAR ISLAND

Tern
Nesting
Area

Abandoned
Lighthouse

tide rips

Gunpowder
Cove

Magnus's
Camp

rocks

breakers

Outer
Point

tide rips

THRUMCAP ISLAND

rocks

tide rips

ATLANTIC OCEAN

1   2   3   4
Nautical Miles

Chapter One

"Come on, boy. You can do it."

My dog Pogo stands with his toes spread wide in the sand, smiling at me. He looks from me to the boat. His tail gives a halfhearted wag.

"Come on, now," I say, trying to steady my voice so he won't detect just how desperate I am to get going. "Want a treat? I'll give you a treat when you get in. Come on."

His tail makes a more enthusiastic wag, but he still doesn't budge.

Daylight is spreading from the east, the fog parting to show the fading stars between wisps. The blurry forms of boats appear—ones that were invisible when I rowed out to the mooring to sail the boat back for Pogo. Wavelets splash on the shore at my feet. The water is silky and cool around my ankles. We have to get going before full daylight arrives or we'll be spotted.

"Come on." I try to make my voice sound firm without being threatening. "Let's stop with the games." I sigh and toss the mainsheet into the cockpit of *Scallop*, our catboat. The sail slaps in the slack air.

"Okay, boy. I want you to cooperate."

I step across the sand to him. Still smiling, he tips up his grizzled chin as I grip his harness. The moment I pull, he digs his paws into the sand. I lean harder toward the boat. The harness slides around his head. "Don't do this to me, boy," I say. "We have to get going. C'mon, you *like* to sail."

I dig into my shorts pocket and pull out one of the soft treats he loves. I hold it out over the cockpit. "Pogo," I say. "Come."

A gull coasts overhead, taking its sweet time, and I see it peer down at the treat as if marking it for later.

I wave the treat back and forth. Pogo doesn't know what's going on, doesn't know we have to get away, doesn't know what my parents have planned for him.

I walk back up and offer him the treat. "I forgot, boy. You can't see it very well, can you?"

He lifts his snout and I hold the treat just away from him. He moves down the beach, following my hand. Drool loops out of his mouth.

"In you go." I grip his harness and haul him over the side into the boat, his toenails clattering on the deck. "Good boy. Now sit."

He doesn't sit. I have to push down on his hindquarters. He sniffs the duffel bag, then the backpack, scenting the food inside.

"Okay. Now we can shove off."

I hold out the treat and he presses his muzzle against my hand. He vacuums up the treat. "Good boy." I wipe my hand on my shorts.

I shove off and climb in. "Right." I sit down and pat his head. "We're off."

He turns, his smile making me smile, and his tail thumps once on the deck.

Chapter Two

The clear sky of dawn gives way to haze as the sun climbs. The breeze gets us out beyond Thrumcap Island, the small island midway between Fog Island and Malabar, before it quits and we lose headway and bob on water as smooth as sheet metal a mile from Malabar.

"Don't worry, boy. We'll get there."

I glance behind us. The low biscuit-colored dunes of Fog Island lie along the horizon. The morning has worn on and I can see two white flecks—the bow wakes of boats coming out of Fog Island Harbor and moving off on their courses.

Pogo is flaked out on the deck, snoring like a distant foghorn. I see his paws twitching as I let my arm dangle over the tiller, my legs stretched out in front of me.

I'm not worried—that we'll make it to Malabar, that is. Really, I'm not worried.

The sail droops back and forth, sliding a shadow over us one minute, letting the sun pour down on us the next.

"We need to get moving," I whisper. "Come on, breeze, before someone sees us."

Pogo lifts his head and peers at me.

"You okay, boy?"

He begins panting, his pink tongue curling, and puts his head back down on the deck. I pull the duffel bag to me and take out Pogo's canteen—a plastic water bowl with a screw-on lid.

"Thirsty, Pogo? I don't want you to get parched." But he

starts snoring again, probably lulled by the easy motion of the boat. I put the canteen away.

I'm not lulled.

I look across the water, its surface glaring in the brassy sunshine, and a flare of heat rises in my chest when I think back to what I heard last night.

I didn't mean to be eavesdropping. They didn't mean to be overheard. My parents were out on the screened-in porch. I was up in my room above them, the windows wide open to catch the air.

The foghorn mooing kept me up—that and my sweat. Then a great horned owl started *hoo-hoo, hoo-hoo-hoo*ing in the big pine behind the house as if it were answering the foghorn. Standing at the window, at least, I was cooler thanks to the fog coming through the screen. Below, I heard my parents murmuring. I listened to the owl, and then the foghorn, and then I strained harder to catch what my father was saying.

"I'm afraid," he said, "that Pogo has reached the end of the trail."

I felt as though if I moved a hole would open up below me and I would drop into it. I didn't breathe.

"Do you really think it's time?" my mom said.

I didn't want to hear the answer.

Dad sighed. "I hate to say it, but I'm afraid so. We've tried everything."

I waited. Mom said nothing. I heard the owl, then the foghorn.

Then she said, "But look at him. Lying there so content."

"He's fifteen years old, hon," said Dad. "That's ancient for a dog his size. We don't want to wait till he's in pain—too much pain. How much longer can we put it off? He hobbles. He has trouble lying down. And every morning, another present. Every night, another—"

"Don't remind me." She paused, then said, "I suppose you're right."

"It's about his quality of life," Dad went on. "We've been over this again and again. We don't want him to suffer, do we? Ever. The vet said it was inoperable."

Mom was silent a long time. The owl must have flown away because now I heard only the foghorn.

Then she said just loud enough to hear, "We don't have any choice, I guess." She sighed. "But what about Sam? Pogo's his . . ." Her voice sounded squeezed. "How much more can we . . ." On the last word her voice broke so it creaked like an old door hinge.

She went silent. I felt my windpipe swell. I didn't want her to say it.

"We can't think about that," said Dad. "This is different." The foghorn moaned. "We have to think about Pogo. Just about Pogo."

I listened. I heard a rocking chair shift. The foghorn sounded.

"In the morning," said Dad finally, his voice low. "In the morning I'll call the vet."

"No," I whispered to myself. "I am not going to let this happen."

I went back to bed. I waited, listening to the foghorn, until I heard their rocking chairs scrape on the wood planks of the porch and the front door close. I heard them squeak up the stairs and go into their room. The whole time, my heart whirled around in my chest like it was looking for a way to get out. Then I got up.

I found my duffel bag and my waterproof backpack in my closet. I stuffed a couple of shirts and shorts and a pair of khakis and a sweatshirt into the duffel and my watch and phone and handheld GPS into the backpack.

Then I sat beside the window, waiting, counting out the moans of the foghorn.

I heard no sound in the house. I stretched out on my back on the floor, and I thought about Pogo, sleeping downstairs on his bed, unknowing.

I thought of all our years together—how he was always

there, my brother's dog but like another older brother to me. I thought of when I was little, building sand castles, and Pogo getting his head stuck in a plastic bucket. I thought of us exploring the marshes and thickets and woods. I thought of him sailing with Steve and me, building snow forts and biting snowballs, always smiling, smiling, never having a bad day. I thought of him getting the scampers when he was excited and crouching down and pinning his ears back and running around the house, my mom yelling at him to stop but laughing, too. I thought of Steve teaching him to balance a treat on the end of his nose and how Pogo would look cross-eyed at it before he flipped it up and ate it. I thought of Dad chanting "What a vicious yellow Lab, looking for a sock to nab" when Pogo used to tear apart our socks. I thought of Steve right before he left, telling me to take care of Pogo, saying that he was my dog now.

And then I fell asleep.

I dreamed of running over the water, Pogo bounding ahead of me, Steve running out ahead faster and faster till he was a speck on the horizon. I dreamed of trying to wake up. I dreamed that I was dreaming of waking up. And then I did wake up.

I heard the foghorn. Crickets chirped.

Gray light was in the window.

I had to get moving. Fast. But I couldn't run. I pulled on my hat and picked my way down the stairs, duffel slung over my shoulder, backpack in hand. The stairs creaked. I paused each time to listen. No other sound came from the house but the *tock* of the clock downstairs.

I moved faster once I got downstairs. Pogo lifted his head as I passed him on my way into the kitchen. "Good boy," I whispered. "I'll be right back."

In the pantry I grabbed his bag of dry food and shoved it into the backpack along with his arthritis pills. I found his canteen and filled it with water, took a gallon jug of water for myself and put those in the duffel. Then I jammed in a box of cereal, a jar of peanut butter, a loaf of bread and a box of granola bars for me. I started out and then ducked back to grab a bag of his treats and a couple of oranges from the basket on the kitchen table. I knew we'd need more food, but that was what the handline on the boat was for—fishing.

Already the sky was lighter.

"Let's go, boy," I whispered to Pogo. "No time to waste."

He lifted his head and smiled, and I bent down to haul him up. He scrabbled off his bed and wobbled upright.

"Good boy," I whispered as I led him toward the front door. I glanced over my shoulder, back at the fireplace. The folded flag on the mantel was only a dim triangle in the faint light.

Malabar Island lies a mile across the water, tantalizing me, its dunes and scrub-covered hills beckoning but out of reach.

If only I had an outboard. But not on *Scallop*. She has never has an outboard, and she never will, not if Dad has his way. Looks like I'll have to paddle.

I sit back in the cockpit. Ahead, the lumpy dunes of the island are the last landform before the open ocean. Behind us, Thrumcap Island is a bristly hump. Fog Island is only a smudge in the growing haze.

The sail hangs lazy and listless. I squint up at the sun. The boom swings one way, then the other, as if sniffing the air for a breeze. The shadow of the sail slips over me, then slides away so sunshine bakes down. The rigging rattles.

I hear the spearing call of a tern—and Pogo's snoring. I see the knife-winged bird fly past, peering down onto the slick surface of the water as if at its own reflection.

"Come on, breeze." My words are swallowed in the openness. "We're so close."

When I look behind us again, I have to blink. Clouds I hadn't seen because of the haze are spreading toward us fast.

Above the smudge of Fog Island, the horizon is dark. The water has taken on an oily sheen.

"Okay, boy." I reach under the foredeck. "Time to move."

I grab the paddle and Pogo raises his head and cocks his ears. I jab the paddle into the water just as I hear the first growl of thunder in the distance.

Chapter Three

I take three strokes on the starboard side. The boat pushes ahead, but swerves off to port.

I hop over Pogo to the port side and take three more strokes to bring the boat back the other way. Then I hop back over Pogo again to repeat the process. We're not making much headway toward the island. The tide or a current could be setting us off course.

Each time I leap over him Pogo turns his head with me, watching me, panting in the heat. He probably thinks this is some sort of game. It's no game—not with those clouds approaching.

They're lumpy clouds. Steve told me once that they're called mammatus clouds, and that when you see them, expect to get clobbered by a squall. They're spreading overhead, looking like evil Ping-Pong balls pushing out the bottom of a silver cloud. A severe thunderstorm will hit soon.

"You should have seen the one that hit us last night," Steve wrote to me when he first got deployed. "I saw continuous lightning for thirty minutes. What a welcoming committee."

"Let's get you out of the way," I say, panting as much as Pogo in the thick air. I put the paddle down, hoist Pogo up and lead him over to the stern rail, his toenails clicking on the planks.

When he was younger I could have told him to go sit by the stern, and he would have hopped up and obeyed. But now he's not as sharp as he used to be.

"Now stay, okay, boy?"

He leans against the rail, watching me, his pink tongue bobbing, his hind legs splayed out.

I go back to paddling. Now I can move back and forth faster. I can see we're gaining on the island. As I paddle, the light dims to a greenish dusk. I smell a faint odor of scorched rubber—ozone. Thunder grumbles behind us.

Then I feel it.

Air washes against my face. I look overboard and see the green water surface shiver. The boom swings and I duck down.

"Look, Pogo!" I stow the paddle beneath the foredeck, then grab the tiller and haul in the sheet. "A breeze! This is more like it."

The sail fills and *Scallop* surges ahead. The water gurgles in our wake and we begin to heel. Behind us the sky darkens. Thunder echoes across the water.

When you're on the open water in a small boat, nothing muffles the sound of thunder. It's an immense sound, rolling over you like hundreds of invisible bulldozers crashing into each other, then echoing, echoing, echoing.

The breeze strengthens. A puff of air lifts Pogo's ears. He narrows his eyes and sniffs the breeze.

"Hang on." The boat heels harder. "We're almost there."

I see the long, low beach at the southernmost tip of Malabar dead ahead. It's called Outer Point, and it's not where we want to land. It's where Fog Island Sound meets the Atlantic Ocean. The currents and tide and the long swells rolling in make it too dangerous.

We're so close now I can hear the low boom of the surf and the cries of the gulls piercing the air as they lift off the beach at our approach. We have to change course and run along the shore.

"Ready about," I call. "Hard alee!" I pull the tiller toward me and the bow swings around through the wind. The sail goes slack and slaps and rattles until the boom slams around and the wind catches the sail on the other side.

Pogo slips toward the tiller as his side of the boat tips up, his paws planted on the deck but his toenails not gripping. I reach out, haul him around the tiller and pull him beside me. "There you go." I hold on to the tiller as the wind strengthens. His tail thumps against the deck.

The sight of a snake-tongue of lightning flickering in the blackness over the water sends chills over me. The tiller gets heavier in the rising wind, and I have to ease the sheet so I can handle the sail. Chop springs up on the water, and the boat bucks through the steeper waves, throwing spray over us.

Thunder tears the air overhead. I spot what looks like a narrow inlet bordered by rock-strewn sand spits, and I bring *Scallop* around to head for it. A gust heels us over hard, and I have to grab Pogo's harness to keep him from sliding across the deck.

In the strong wind we're bounding across the water, and soon we're passing the first spit. A streak of lightning sizzles down behind us, chased by an explosion of thunder. More lightning spiders along the bottoms of the clouds.

As soon as we're inside the inlet, I head for the closest beach. "We're going straight in," I tell Pogo. "Hold on."

I can see shells and rocks and seaweed and ridges of sand on the bottom now. I pull the centerboard up so we can slip right onto the beach.

"Here we go." I let the sheet fly out of my hand so the sail spills the wind as the bow is driven onto the sand. We come to a stop with a crunch. The following waves crash against our hull. I jump up to drop the sail, and it piles down over top of us.

I fight to furl it and lash it to the boom. I haul the anchor out from beneath the foredeck and toss it up onto the beach, then return to hoist Pogo out of the cockpit.

The first drops of rain smack against us like cold bullets.

"We'll come back for the gear. Let's see if we can find some shelter first."

Pogo is standing in the wave wash, relieving himself, looking up at me as if to say *I can't help it. That was one long boat ride.*

The rain bites down on us, harder now, and I can feel it crack on the top of my cap.

"Ready?"

At last we shuffle off the beach, lightning forking into the sea behind us, and head away from the water through a stand of small pines and underbrush.

"Maybe we should just get down underneath some of these bushes till it's over," I say, pushing through the thicket. Pogo's way behind, his nose glued to a tuft of grass. "Come on, boy!" I shout. I clap my hands. "This is no time for sniffing." I have to run back for him, grab his harness, and pull him with me. "Must be a pretty amazing smell."

We step out of the thicket into a clearing, and right before us stands an old plank camp with a shingle roof, not much bigger than a garden shed.

Then the downpour lets loose.

"Let's give it a try," I shout over the rush of rain. We go up the warped wooden steps onto the porch. The planks give under our weight.

I knock on the wooden door. "Hello! Anyone there?"

Another explosion of thunder helps me decide to try the door. It opens.

I look back at Pogo. He's soaked, wincing as the raindrops splat on his head.

I push the door open wider. "Let me take a look first." I step inside but he doesn't wait to follow, bumping into the back of my legs and pushing past me.

In the gloom Pogo shakes, flinging water everywhere. The rain drums on the roof and lightning flashes in the windows, for a moment showing me the rough room. I have to blink to believe what I saw by the flash of the lightning. Yes, in the corner of the room is a tree trunk. Another flash shows me that it is a real live tree growing out of the floor and through the roof.

Pogo ambles over to sniff it.

I'm not sure if the place is inhabited, even though I can now make out a cot in the corner, a floor-to-ceiling cabinet on one wall and a woodstove made out of a steel drum with a pipe leading out through the roof. I see a lantern hanging from a rafter, and I catch a whiff of kerosene.

Just then the door bangs open behind me.

I whirl around.

Stepping through the doorway is a huge figure, and I stutter-step backward, my heart whirring.

Lightning flares behind the figure and thunder blasts around us. In the flash I can see that it's a giant of a man with strands of snowy hair beneath a rumpled straw hat with a round brim. His eyes are such a pale blue that they seem to be circles of sky. He's holding a big fish by the gills in one hand and a fishing pole in the other and has a bird sitting on his shoulder—a tern.

The tern flaps its wings and chitters at us.

"I've had birds and beasts of all kinds in my place before," says the giant in a voice as low and gravelly as thunder itself, "but I've never had an elf and his dog. What are you doing in here, boy?"

Chapter Four

My jaw has become steel. I can't open or close it.

Lightning flashes blue behind the giant and thunder pounds down.

He shoves the door with his heel and it swings shut. He sets the pole in the corner and tips his hat back on his head.

Pogo hobbles toward him.

"Po—Pogo!" He doesn't stop. What if he has decided in his old age to become an attack dog and sink his teeth into the giant?

But I don't have to worry. He dips his head and slinks toward the man, his tail revolving like a propeller.

The giant looks down at Pogo. He lays the fish on the plank floor and lowers himself, folding his long body to squat down. The tern flutters its wings. The giant eases his huge hands out as if he is going to catch a baby. "Now, who is this fine specimen of a Labrador?" he says in a warm tone. And what accent is that? German? "An old gentleman—someone with as many years as me." He looks from Pogo to me and back to Pogo.

Pogo touches his snout to the giant's hands, drawn to the fish scent.

"Maybe you can tell me," the giant says, taking Pogo's head in his hands and lifting it to look into his eyes, "what the name of your young friend is."

The rain comes on even harder now, shattering on the roof like a load of gravel poured from the clouds. A gust of wind shakes the walls and rattles the windows.

"I'm Sam," I whisper. The giant looks at me and cocks an eyebrow. "Sam," I say louder. "Sam Pendleton. That's my dog. Pogo. We can leave now. We were just trying to—"

The giant raises a hand. "No apologies. You were trying to get out of the storm. In such an emergency, my castle"—he sweeps his arm around—"is yours."

The giant seems to mean us no harm—though I don't like being cornered. I tell myself to say nothing more. I have to figure out a way to escape. A giant living in a shack on a desert island is not to be trusted. But I can't burst past him and run off into the storm.

He passes one of his large hands over Pogo's head and rubs his right ear. His hand stops just below the ear. He tilts his head. I can tell he feels it—the lump. Then he stands up.

Pogo looks up at him and bounds up and down on his forepaws, the trick Steve taught him that showed how well his name fit: his pogo-stick bounce.

"I wish I had a treat for you," the giant says. He reaches down and pats Pogo on the head again. Pogo lowers his haunches and sits down beside him. He looks back at me. He wants to tell me something. His tail thumps on the floorboards. He gazes back up at the giant and edges closer to him and smiles. He pushes his shoulder against the giant's leg, then looks back at me. He's trying to tell me the giant is okay.

"This," says the giant, pointing at the tern, "is Fuego. And I am Magnus Fisker."

"Thanks for . . . thanks for letting us use your place. I didn't think anyone lived here."

"Quite the contrary," he says. "Many creatures have at one time or another lived here, though at the moment the only residents—besides some field mice, crickets, and assorted other small creatures—are a lame-winged *Sterna paradisaea* and one ancient *Homo sapiens*. That would be Fuego and me. But we're all soaked. Let me build a fire before we take a chill."

The storm throws down more lightning and thunder. Rain

hisses on the roof. I can hear the wind ripping through the pines. The shed trembles. Rainwater churns like suds on the windows.

Magnus puts the fish in the sink by the bigger window. Then he pumps a handle that brings water out of a spigot, and rinses the fish and his hands.

The place is a lot more furnished than I first thought it was. A small wooden table sits in front of the side window and a desk stands beside the cot.

"Fishing for this fine specimen is what caused us to be caught in the storm," he says, drying his hands on a dish towel. "Perhaps you'll join us in what is the best meal known to mankind—striped bass fresh from the ocean."

He glances at me. I love striped bass. My stomach creaks with hope. In my rush to escape with Pogo neither one of us had a bite before we left.

"But first things first," Magnus says. From a wooden box on the floor beside the woodstove he pulls out a couple of sheets of newspaper, crumples them up and puts them into the stove. Then, from the same box, he takes a handful of pinecones and sets them on the paper. He takes three lengths of firewood from a wire clam basket and sets them on top. I begin to shiver in my wet clothes as he strikes a match and lights the paper. I'm hoping that fire catches soon. Pogo is shivering, too.

Magnus goes to the cabinet and pulls a folded wool blanket off a shelf. He tosses it to me. "Dry him off while I tend to the fire," he says. "We don't want the old salt catching cold. There's a bowl below the sink for water."

He bends down in front of the stove, leans forward and blows on the flames. "So tell me, Sam Pendleton," he says. "What brings you and your old friend to the island?"

Fuego flaps his wings and swivels his head around to me just as another blast of thunder shakes the windows.

Chapter Five

I busy myself with drying Pogo. Out of the corner of my eye I can see that Fuego is still looking at me. "There, boy." I crouch down beside him and rub his back with the blanket, the skunky odor of wet dog thick in my nostrils. I drape the blanket over his head to dry his forehead and ears. "That feels better, doesn't it?"

He smiles up at me, peering out from the flap of the blanket like a monk.

I know I can't pretend I didn't hear the question. I figure the longer I wait the less believable any answer will be. "Just out for a sail," I say. "I've been wanting to sail to Malabar for a long time. We live on Fog Island."

That's the truth. My dad and Steve sailed out here early last summer—with Pogo—and camped for the night. I couldn't go. I couldn't go because I'd broken my arm jumping off the pier and Mom said "under no circumstances" was I to go camping on a desert island with my arm in a cast whether I was with my father and brother or not. My brother wouldn't have let a broken arm stop him—or Mom or Dad or anything else. He would have laughed the whole thing off and sailed away. I wish I could have been like that.

The fire pops and Pogo presses his head between my knees. He hates when fires make sharp sounds.

"It's okay, boy. It's just a fire. It'll warm you up."

Does Magnus believe me? Maybe if I ask him a question

first, he'll move on to another subject. "Do you live here all year round?"

Thunder cracks like a massive tree split down the middle, but this time it's no longer right overhead. The rain keeps rushing down heavy as a waterfall. I hear a drip coming from the tree.

"All spring, summer and fall," he says, cramming more newspaper into the woodstove. "In winter only part of the time. My daughter insists I stay with her during the worst of the winter gales—weather I dearly love out here. Though Fuego doesn't mind the warmer climate."

"Must be cold—cold and windy."

He straightens up, taking his time, holding one hand to his back. He exhales. "Nothing walking and a woodstove can't handle. Though my right ankle keeps reminding me of what I did to it when I was your age." He raises his right leg and flexes his foot, then moves to the sink and holds the fish up by the tail.

The arm I broke flexes all by itself. The doctor said it healed, but sometimes I still get a queasy feeling that the bone is ready to snap again.

"And now to filet this beauty and prepare our meal. You must be hungry after such a long sail—a voyage worthy of Magellan for a young man and an old dog." He takes a wooden-handled knife with a thin, curved blade from beside the sink, flicks it down the back of the fish and slices off a filet in about five seconds flat. Then he flips the fish over onto the other side and does the same. He skins the filets and pumps out water to rinse them.

He cuts a sliver of flesh from one of the filets and holds it out for Fuego. Fuego pecks toward it. "Easy," says Magnus. Fuego waits, looking at Magnus. Magnus nods. Only then does Fuego pluck it from his fingers.

I wonder how long it took Magnus to train Fuego to do his fish-eating trick. Steve worked with Pogo for about a month on his treat-on-the-nose trick before Pogo learned to wait and not just shake his head and gobble the treat right away.

"What kind of boat do you have?" Magnus clatters a cast-iron fry pan on the stove top. "Where did you put in?" He pours oil into the pan and crouches to check the fire. He pulls a stick from the basket and pokes the fire with it. Then he stands up and lays the filets into the pan. The fish sizzles.

I drape the blanket around my shoulders and step closer to the fire. The warmth pulses out and I can feel it warming my bones.

Thunder booms again, this time farther away.

"My boat's a twelve-and-a-half-foot catboat. She's in a cove not far from here."

"That you enter through a narrow cut between two rocky points?"

I nod. "Our supplies are still aboard."

I stop but I know I've made a mistake—a big one. I glance at him. He leans over the fry pan and pokes the fish with a fork.

"That's Gunpowder Cove," he says. "Did you see another boat there, a rowing skiff?"

"No."

He chuckles. "That's good—it's my boat. A seventeen-foot wood lapstrake skiff I built years ago. I hide it in the same cove, up in the brush. Oh, I keep an outboard and a radio for emergencies, true. But rowing on the waves, only the sounds of the sea and the birds around you, that is the life."

"Why do you hide it?"

He flips one filet and it lands with a hiss. Pogo steps forward, twitching his nose. Fuego flaps his wings. "Force of habit," says Magnus. "I grew up hiding things, even myself. When I was a boy, even younger than you, my parents and sister and brother and I lived in the woods."

"What woods? Around here?"

"In Denmark. That's my homeland. This was during the

war, when the Nazis occupied my country, and my father—who like was me an ornithologist—wrote some things that were published in a newspaper that the Nazis did not like. We had to live in the woods and on the beaches—which were much like the ones on this island—far from our home in Copenhagen. I got used to hiding what I wanted to keep."

He flips the other filet. The rain has become a soft patter on the roof. The window facing the west has become lighter.

"To me, it was the greatest time of my life. To escape the Nazis was a game to me. Not so for my parents, of course. But to live outdoors in the open air or in huts was an adventure. It made me want to follow my father's path, be among the animals and birds, have the sky as my roof."

He looks out the window. "Not that living outside," he says, "doesn't have its hazards. I once jumped into a ditch to avoid a German armored vehicle. They didn't see me but I fractured my talus—my anklebone. The pain . . ." He rolls his eyes, grimacing, and shakes his head.

I know, I almost say. *I know about the pain.*

He pokes one of the filets with the fork. "Almost done."

He turns to me, holding the fork in his big hand. "You said you had supplies," he says, just as a beam of sunlight pours through the window. "Are you off on a long voyage, or are you planning to stay on the island?"

Chapter Six

I'm really cornered now. I don't know what to say. I can't tell him the truth.

"On a long voyage. Well, maybe not that long. I just wanted to sail out here and beyond to . . ." Now I'm getting my story mixed up. I have to scramble to think of where I wanted to sail. "I was going to stay on the island and then sail out to the wreck—you know, the one off to the northeast of here?—and then sail home. My father and brother went out there last year, the same trip when they camped on Malabar, before Steve went over—" I catch myself again. I hold my hand up to shield my eyes from the sunlight—and from Magnus's eyes. I have to stop saying so much. "It's just that I've always wanted to. Go out there, I mean."

One of Magnus's bushy white eyebrows is raised. Is he about to burst out laughing or accuse me of being a liar? He doesn't say anything for a moment. Then he tilts his head. "I see," he says. "With your old friend."

Pogo wags his tail.

Magnus smiles. "What do you say we eat al fresco," he says, "out in the air? The storm is passing. I trust Pogo would like a portion, too."

Great idea—we can eat and then make our getaway.

He loads three plates with fish and hands two to me. I follow him out, noticing that he has a hitch as he walks. Pogo hobbles behind me with his nose to one of the plates. We stand on the wet boards of the creaky porch.

The air is still thick with moisture, and steam rises from the beach grass on the dunes as the sun pours down. Overhead the trailing clouds of the storm are pulling away, the low black scraps looking like they're hustling to keep up with the rest of the storm. Above the trees to the west the sky is showing blue. The water droplets on the needles of the scrub pines sparkle in the sun and the sound of dripping is like countless little lips smacking. Thunder mumbles somewhere far to the east.

Magnus has cut up Pogo's portion.

"Here you go, boy," I say. "Bet you're starving. You haven't had anything—" I stop before I make another mistake.

I set the plate down on the boards and Pogo is on it before I take my hand away. I sneak a glance at Magnus. He's holding up a fleck of fish for Fuego.

"What kind of a name is Fuego?" I say, trying to cover my tracks.

Magnus holds a forkful of fish above his plate. "Arctic terns make amazing journeys every year—the longest migration of any bird—thousands of miles from here to South America. One of the spots where they go is the very tip, Tierra del Fuego, the land of fire. When I rescued Fuego, I thought the name would be fitting, considering how fiery he was. He did not like being cared for."

I take a bite of the fish. The moment it hits my mouth, I realize how starved I am. "What did you rescue him from?"

"I found him on the other side of the dune, not far from Gunpowder Cove. That's a tern nesting site. He was only about two years old, just mature enough to find a mate. His wing was broken—bitten, from the looks of it. I'm not sure how. Perhaps a gull or a fox. Normally I would have let nature take its course, but I made an unscientific decision to save him. His bone was shattered and alas it never healed well enough for him to fly again. His life took him on a different path. Did you know that terns can live into their twenties, and that the oldest one recorded was thirty-four years old?"

I shake my head as I shovel the fish in. I think about my arm and the pain shooting through it even when I held it like it was made of glass as I hurried home, dripping wet. Mine was only a hairline fracture, and I know how much that hurt. Imagine Fuego's pain.

Pogo is licking his plate, sliding it across the deck, his tail bouncing with pleasure. Then he turns and takes two steps toward me, his snout raised to gauge what might be left on my plate, and he stumbles, his hindquarters crumbling, and flops on the planks.

"Get up, boy." I grab his harness with one hand and lift him, then glance at Magnus. He's watching Pogo.

"Arthritis," he says. "Almost inevitable in one as old as Pogo."

Magnus finishes his fish, leaving a small chunk, and bends down to set the plate on the porch. "Here you go, Pogo. Would you mind polishing this off for me?" Pogo vacuums up the fish and licks the plate.

Fuego chitters and flaps his wings. "Don't be jealous," says Magnus.

I set my plate on the boards. "How old is Fuego?" I ask as Pogo scours my plate.

Magnus twists his head around to the bird and grins. "He's been sentenced to living with me now for about thirteen years, so I'd say he's fifteen or so. Which means he's getting to be an old codger like me." He stoops to pick up the plates. "How old is Pogo?"

"Fifteen," I blurt out. Now he's bound to wonder why I'm taking a long trip with such an old dog. "Same age as Fuego."

Magnus nods. "Let me put these in the sink and then we'll go check on the terns before we get your supplies—unless you've decided to shove off on your voyage." He disappears through the door.

Pogo lets out a groan as he lies down. He laps a paw, then the other—his after-meal cleanup. I'm beginning to wonder if taking off with him was such a good idea. Maybe he doesn't want to be dragged all over the ocean for . . . for what? He seems happy lying there, and maybe that's all he really wants to do. Maybe he'd be happier at home. But if we had stayed at home . . . I didn't have any choice.

"Ready?" Magnus comes back out on the porch. He now has a kind of telescope hanging from a strap around his neck. "We'll see how the fledglings fared in the storm."

Chapter Seven

"Part of what I do," says Magnus, "is gauge the success of the tern colony every summer. The chicks hatched several weeks ago. Now they're mature enough to get ready to fly."

We're standing on top of the dune beyond his camp. The sun beats down hot now, and the storm has disappeared out to sea beyond the eastern horizon. The rain has released the scent of salty rot from the beach and the spice of sap from the scrub pines. The beach stretches away to the north. To the south lie the cove and *Scallop*.

"Down there among those rocks is where the terns nest," he says, pointing. "Do you see the birds flying around above? If we get too close, they'll come after us. I've had many a tern try to peck through my hat, Fuego included. The storm has disrupted them enough, so we'll keep our distance."

He raises the scope. I can hear tern calls like squeaky gears as the birds flutter above the beach. Fuego flaps and chitters in answer.

"The eggs look like speckled stones," says Magnus. "It's a wonder that terns can hatch their eggs. They lay them in a shallow scrape right on the sand or bare rock. Then they hatch and the young look like dirty puffs of lint. They're fledging now, meaning they're getting ready to fly." He sweeps the scope farther up the beach. Then he stops. He holds the scope away, blinking, then sets it to his eye again. "I was afraid this might happen."

"What?"

All I can see are the birds flying around like origami come to life above the sand and rocks, flicking blade shadows over the ground.

"One of the young ones."

"What happened?"

He lowers the scope and shakes his head. "Difficult to tell. A hawk, a gull, even the storm could have gotten it." He hands me the scope. "Take a look if you'd like. You'll see a red flag—the closest one. That's to mark where eggs were. The carcass of the young tern is lying just this side of it—right by where its nest was."

I train the scope on the beach and bring the red flag into focus. I search the rocks and sand and find the bird. The scope is so powerful the body of the tern fills the lens. It doesn't have the black cap of the ones I see flapping around in the air. It's scruffier, speckled more like the rocks it's lying on. It looks lonely lying there, a slender pod of folded wing feathers that will never fly.

Magnus pulls a notebook out of his pants pocket and scribbles in it with a pencil. "The terns are suffering a lot from predation this year," he says. "But I suspect this one died in the storm."

I lower the scope and look at Pogo. He's lying down and panting in the sun, his pink tongue lolling. I think about what a long life he's had compared to the young tern.

I hand the scope back to Magnus. "Too bad the tern didn't get a chance," I say, "to fly to Tierra del Fuego. Too bad it had to die so young."

He nods. "It is," he says. "But birds do not distinguish between living and dying as we do. A tern fights to live, and will defend its nest and young, but it has a different relationship with death. From the many years I've lived among the terns, I know that they live when it's time to live and they die when it's time to die. Animals understand this better than humans."

I look down at my dog. *Why did you have to get so old?* I think. *Why couldn't you stay young? Do you miss Mom and Dad? Do you miss Steve?*

"How long," says Magnus, "have you had your friend here?"

I should not talk about Pogo or I might give too much away. "He's always been with us," I say. "I mean I wasn't born yet when we got him, but he's the first thing I remember. I remember him splashing in the bathtub with me once when my mom was giving me a bath. He climbed right in."

"So you've been together all your lives."

I nod. "We've done everything together." My voice cracks before I can stop it, the storm breaking inside me. I take a breath and go on. "He sails with me. He goes fishing with me. He hikes with me. Well, not so much now, but he used to. He used to swim and swim and swim. But now . . ."

Magnus says nothing. I wonder if he can read my mind. He waits. The terns call in the air.

"Now they want to put him down."

Still he says nothing.

"And I thought I could take him away, bring him out here, find a place to hide, take care of him the way Steve said, and then it wouldn't happen."

I look up at Magnus. He's looking out at the terns. Then he crouches down, tips his hat back and calls Pogo. Pogo struggles to his feet. He sets his ears back, dips his head and shuffles toward Magnus, his tail swinging low.

Magnus takes Pogo's face in his hands and lifts it up. "Your friend Sam here has done a noble thing. He saved your life. Now he needs your help. You need to tell him what to do—what you want him to do. What is that, Pogo? Do you want to stay out here on the island, go on a voyage, or do you want to be back home with all your family? What would make you happy?"

The tip of Pogo's tail twitches back and forth. His hind legs sway. I see him lift his eyes to me.

Maybe I haven't been fair to him. Does he want to be home, no matter what that might mean? Is he in pain? Maybe I should have talked to Mom and Dad.

Magnus pats Pogo on the top of the head and rises. Pogo saunters over to a clump of beach grass, presses his nose against it and begins snuffling.

"I can walk with you to your boat if you like," Magnus says. "You have plenty of daylight left if you head straight back."

The storm inside me has broken and passed and left me feeling empty. I look back at Pogo. His hind legs have given way and he's sitting on his rump, looking around as if to ask what happened.

I look down at the cove where *Scallop* lies waiting on the beach. I know the choice I have to make.

All I can do is call for Pogo to follow me down the dune.

Chapter Eight

Pogo is stretched out on the cockpit planks in a pool of sunshine. He's snoring and grunting, his paws twitching, probably worn out from the trek over the dunes. The shadow of the sail drifts over him as I point the boat away from the island. I look behind us. Magnus is on the beach, watching as the distance between us grows, a small figure now against the rocks and sand, so far away I can't see Fuego. I wave one last time. I see his long arm sweep once, twice, like a human windshield wiper.

The direction of the breeze makes us set a course toward Outer Point first before we can make the long tack back toward Fog Island. I don't really mind. I don't want to rush back. Does Pogo?

I think back to the conversation Mom and Dad were having, and I wonder if I was wrong to think they were talking about ending Pogo's life—right away, that is. Dad said that he'd call the vet. Did he mean that he would ask the vet's opinion what to do? Maybe the vet will try some other kind of treatment. Maybe Pogo has a chance after all. Maybe.

We pass the end of Outer Point. Gulls swarm the sky, jeering and flapping. I can hear the low boom of surf on the beach on the ocean side of the island, a sound that makes me want to go take a look at what's beyond. The wreck.

Excitement ripples through me: The wreck that Dad and Steve sailed to lies out there. It's supposed to be about ten or eleven miles northeast of the island, aground in the shoals where so many vessels went down over the years. Steve told me how haunting it was to sail around a ship sticking out of the ocean, all alone out there with only the swells echoing through the hull.

"I'll remember that feeling," Steve told me. "I'll remember that forever."

We still have all afternoon to make the sail back home. If we sneak out around Outer Point, I might be able to catch a glimpse of the wreck—if the visibility's good. Could we even get all the way out to it?

"I don't really want to rush back," I say to Pogo. "Do you?"

He's still snoozing. His forepaws make a small paddling motion.

"I'll take that as a no." I bring the boat around on a new heading—due east, into the open ocean. The beach of the point sweeps past. Waves lick the sand with frothy tongues. For a moment we're so close I can see the white litter of shells scattered along the shore. Then the island drops away fast. I still can't see the wreck. I stare out at the horizon. All I can see is the long, slow swells.

I don't want to take us out too far. A few more minutes on this tack, and then we'll come about and head for home. The thought makes my stomach drop. I don't want to turn for home. I want to keep heading out, my dog by my side, into the blue forever.

I turn once more to look back at the island. Goosebumps quiver over me. On its rounded dunes, the spiky tops of the dwarf pine trees are blurring. The green beach grass is going hazy. The sloping beach of Outer Point turns filmy.

I sit upright. "Fog," I whisper. Pogo lifts his head and cocks his ears. I look at him. "Fog, not dog. Look."

Already the entire island is fuzzy.

"Ready about," I call. "Hard alee!" I bring the boat around and set off toward the island. The breeze is light and we skim across the water. I look back behind us. The horizon is no longer visible, a gray ridge replacing it.

"Now's when an outboard would come in handy." Pogo works himself up into a sitting position and looks around, sniffing.

A lone tern wings by overhead and makes its spearing call. I look up. By the time I see it pass over the masthead, it disappears into the fog. When I look in what I think is the direction of the island, I see nothing but a wall of gray fur.

Chapter Nine

Oyster-colored fog surrounds us. The wind has quit. Above the mast I can still see blue sky. The fog billows past. The water clucks against the hull, ripples and dimples on the surface of the gray-green water showing that the tide is taking us somewhere.

I shiver. "We're going to have to wait this out, Pogo."

He is lying down on the planks, his chin cradled on his paws. He doesn't lift his head. He only twitches one eyebrow, then the other, as if to say *Okay, but I kind of liked being back on the island with Magnus and eating striped bass.*

I agree. But we have no choice. If I start paddling now, I could be paddling straight for Ireland. The tide itself could be taking us outward. We could be swept out to the Great South Channel, in the shipping lanes. We could be swept beyond the shipping lanes, far beyond, into the open ocean.

But I've got the GPS. If the fog doesn't lift, I'll take a fix. Still. Getting caught in the fog is a big mistake. Little mistakes breed big ones, especially on a boat, Steve told me.

We have some other gear aboard, too. I duck beneath the foredeck and root through the ditty bag, pushing aside the handline and the first-aid kit.

"Found it." I clutch the boat horn and bring it back with me to the tiller.

Pogo sits up and touches his nose to the canister rim. It's thick with rust.

"Hold your ears." I squint my eyes and squeeze the release as I brace myself for the blast.

No sound comes out. I hear only the lap and gurgle of the water on the hull. I clench the boat horn in one hand and grip the tiller in the other and try to peer through the fog. The top of the masthead is blurred. The blue sky is gone. The walls of fog close in, sealing Pogo and me and the boat in a helmet of gray. I could be at the bottom of a well. I squint to try to penetrate the wall. All I can see is grayness, grayness everywhere.

"Keep your ears open, boy." I train my ears to the distance beyond the fog. The boat seems to be moving, drifting faster than I would have expected. But in which direction? The dimples revolve along the hull to spread in quiet curlicues before disappearing as if absorbed by a gray sponge.

I work the tiller back and forth to scull the boat forward. The splashes and gurgling fill my ears. I won't be able to hear anything else if I keep this up. I relax my hands and listen. Up close, I hear the kiss of the water on the hull. The boom creaks. The gentle wake clucks.

How far, how fast, and where we are drifting, I have no clue.

The currents are now setting us somewhere of their own choosing. They push us with silent, steady hands. The hands might be drawing us into the mouth of the ocean. Time for the GPS.

I sit up straight, then stand in the cockpit.

The boat rocks and sends out a course of small ripples. From the behind us comes a new sound. It's a long blast—a whistle on a boat—followed by two shorter blasts. *A big boat.*

I strain my ears. Now another sound comes to me. It sounds like a whisper, a distant, constant sigh. I listen. The whisper grows into a sizzle. The sizzle is the sound of water being sliced apart by a hull.

I try to see through the fog, to bore through the gray wall to see what is approaching. The watery sizzle is coming closer. Below the sizzle I hear a deeper sound, a low thudding.

"That's some big vessel," I whisper to Pogo.

My heart surges as if jabbed with an electrical charge. My arms and legs fill with air.

It's heading toward us—and it doesn't know we're here. The whistle sounds again, louder, closer.

Chapter Ten

The sizzle becomes the crash of a breaking wave, the thudding a rapid locomotive hammering.

I leap up, the thought of jumping overboard flashing through my mind. But how could I save Pogo if I did?

Shielding my eyes with my hand, I squint, trying to see. Only the sounds come through the gray wall to me. I hold my breath. *Pass by. Maybe it'll just pass by.* But the sounds grow louder, pressing closer.

The blast of the vessel's whistle shivers through me. Should I scream out? Pogo is standing by the port rail, peering ahead, his ears cocked forward. No one will hear me if I scream. Then I see it. The fog begins to part. The wall begins to move, first swaying like a curtain, then swooping faster like a gigantic propeller made of fog.

I feel the air grow heavy and I suck in a long breath and hold it. The thudding and splashing come on, and the fog begins darkening. "This is it, boy. Hold on."

I grab onto the boom with both hands. Then the fog parts as if tent flaps have been flung aside and the tremendous upturned bow of a tugboat with a standing white wave of a bow wake crashing away on either side towers above us and an onrush of air slams us.

I recoil, falling backward onto the rail, then clutch at Pogo's harness and the raised wooden lip of the coaming to keep myself from toppling backward into the water.

The wake crackles and pours past us with the sound of an

avalanche of shattering glass. It grips the boat and spins her around.

I slump to the deck, still holding Pogo's harness. I'm frozen. Fear rises up into me like a scream. I can't move. My legs are splayed out and I pull Pogo to me, to protect him, to protect myself.

Scallop begins to ride up the side of the wake. The rigging goes slack, then snaps and bangs, the sail flapping. The tiller lashes back and forth. I feel the boat yaw and heel and lift. Cold water douses us. Then the boat falls over onto her side and I see a cushion and the backpack slide out from underneath the foredeck. I fling my arms out to grab the backpack but it shoots into the water and gets sucked under the slick black steel of the tug's hull.

I glimpse an orange rust stain on the hull as the wake shoves *Scallop* backward. The tug's horn blasts again in the gloom, and another swell from its stern slaps the boat sideways and spins her around.

I find myself on all fours beside Pogo and look up to see the blurred block letters on the tug's stern: NEPTUNE, PORTLAND.

A swirl of diesel smoke funnels down on us, the harsh stench of burned rubber making me cough. Then an elongated blade slices downward as *Scallop* rides up higher on the wake. I roll over, pulling Pogo with me.

It is not a blade. It is the tow cable stretching from the tug to the barge.

Scallop rises higher. The gaff glances off the cable but the mast hits it, smashing the red flange of the wind indicator mounted on the masthead. I wait for *Scallop* to drop down the side of the wake but she does not. I peer up at the sail. A strand of the cable has come loose and has stabbed the sail just below the gaff, hooking the boat by the sailcloth.

Scallop's bow submarines into the wake and a gush of green water sweeps over the foredeck into the cockpit. Water churns around my ankles and pushes Pogo against me. Another rush of water buckles over the bow. If I don't free the boat, the water will swamp the cockpit as the bow digs in. The mast will break. The boat will go down.

I scrabble my jackknife out of my pocket, flick the blade open and spring to the mast.

"Stay, Pogo!" I see him step after me. "Stay!"

The wooden rings of the sail hoops give me a foothold and I scramble upward, grasping onto the mast, my hands so weak they feel as if they do not belong to me. I look down to see more water slosh over the bow and pour into the cockpit, pushing Pogo aft. He bumps against the stern rail and shakes. "Hold on, boy!"

I look up to see the spline of wire piercing the sail. As I reach upward to thrust the knife into the sailcloth, the boat swerves and my foot slips off the hoop and I swing outward, one hand clamped on a hoop, my mouth open though no sound comes out.

An image of my arm bone buckling flashes through my mind.

The wake shoves the boat hard in the other direction and I swing back and slam against the sail, arm intact. I still grip the knife. Straining to reach up, I stab at the material. The knife glances off. Then I hack at the sail once, twice, three times, splitting the cloth up to the strand of wire, releasing it.

The boat slips free, dropping into the churn of the wake and bucking as if to shake me off. I jump into waves of shin-deep water in the cockpit. Pogo's tail swings back and forth, splashing the surface.

Diving beneath the foredeck, I fumble for the bailer, a plastic juice jug with the top cut off. I thrust aside cushions and the boat hook and the wooden support pole for the cockpit cover and a coil of line but can't find the bailer.

I finally spot it on the other side of the centerboard trunk, floating out from underneath the foredeck. I snatch it up and begin shoveling at the water. The tug's whistle sounds again. Already the tug has disappeared into the fog.

I look behind the boat and go rigid. Looming toward us is the dark form of the barge itself, as wide and tall as a floating warehouse. The barge will crush us, grind right over our little craft, sink us without a shrug.

I drop the bailer and grab the paddle. I lean over the starboard rail, plunging the blade in to drive the boat out of the barge's path. "Stay there, boy!" Pogo presses against the stern rail, his ears laid back, his tail tucked between his legs.

I see the slanted bow rising toward us, and I stab at the water. Stroke after stroke does not seem to move the boat. My lungs burn. My arms quiver. In moments the barge will hit us.

I look up to see the massive shape approaching. A bolt of energy shoots through me. I throw myself into paddling, the surf seething around us.

The barge's hull slams the boat with an impact that knocks us both flat on the deck. Water sloshes over us. I hear a crack and a screech, the boat shivers and whirls around.

Scallop tumbles on the wake and water cascades over us. I lie on my back, clutching the paddle, water pouring like rapids over me. I reach out for Pogo and yank him toward me so he won't float out.

The rusted iron wall of the barge's hull soars above us, then disappears into the heights of the fog.

The boat bangs against the barge again and I shove the paddle against the steel cliff of the hull. The paddle vibrates so hard it stings my hands like a baseball bat hitting a foul on a cold spring day. I push the paddle and *Scallop* spurts away, the gurgle and slosh of the wake in my ears.

Then a curtain of fog closes over the barge. It's gone. Only its wake gurgles and slurps, quieting as the tug heads away, the whistle blasts now weaker.

I sink to my knees on the deck, the water rippling around

us. The boat steadies. We are once again becalmed in the thick fog. Kneeling in the water, clutching the paddle, I begin to quake. The boat floats free. My shuddering begins to calm. We are still alive.

"We made it!"

Pogo looks at me and shakes and steps toward me to lick my ear with his warm, wet tongue.

Chapter Eleven

The GPS. My phone. Pogo's food and pills. My watch—the one I didn't wear because it turned my skin green but that I kept because Steve gave it to me. All of it gone with the backpack. Another setback—a big one. Steve told me that you could navigate by wristwatch if you had to.

"Hold the watch up to the sun at noontime," he said. "The hands at twelve o'clock indicate south. Three is west, nine east. It'll do if you're stuck."

Knowing that won't do me any good now. But I've done what Steve said: "Divide up your supplies. That way you'll never lose everything." I guess he was right. At least we have some food and water.

I feel something brush against my cheek—a puff of air. The sail bells out for a moment, then slackens. Maybe this is it. I take hold of the tiller. Maybe we can get somewhere now. Maybe we're not stuck anymore.

But the breeze does not return.

I start bailing—the water feels colder than I ever felt, icy compared to the warmer waters of the bay where I sail and swim. I haul out the hand pump from beneath the foredeck and set the end of the pipe in the bilge. Then I start pumping, the water gushing out through the hose, splashing overboard. Pogo stands up and peers over, watching, his tail making a slow wave. I pump till only a cupful of water remains between the ribs.

I'm soaked and cold and my canvas boat shoes squish.

Digging back beneath the foredeck, I pull out the khakis and sweatshirt I brought along. I strip off my wet clothes and pull on the dry ones. Much better, even with squishing shoes and soaked hat—the khaki one with the frayed bill and embroidered yellow Lab head and the name Pogo stitched in back, my fave. I wring out the sopping shirt and shorts and stuff them away. This fog is cold. This water is cold.

I know I have to repair the tear in the sail. When the breeze springs up, the sail must be ready to carry us through the tides and currents.

I'm not sure how far we have drifted. At least night's a long way off. Is this how Magnus felt when he was living in the woods in Denmark, unsure what would happen at any time of the day? But Magnus had his family to depend on. I look at Pogo. I'm all he has to depend on—the one who dragged him out here in the first place.

I lower the sail. I have to figure out a way to stitch it up. I stand in the cockpit, holding a pile of sail in my arms with the rest of it draped on the deck. I stare into the fog. Pogo steps on top of the sail, circles once, then again, then again, then again and again, and finally drops down, rests his head on the folds, sighs and closes his eyes.

I stare, and as I stare, I listen to the water smack and tap against the hull. Then, through the grayness, somewhere distant, I hear another rumbling. The sound sends a prickle through me.

Another boat of some kind is out there. This one sounds different from the tug. The engine has a throb, a rumble. The mumbling motor begins to fade almost as soon as I hear it. It heads away from us.

I sit down beside Pogo. My stomach growls. He lifts his head and smiles at me.

We don't have much left to eat. Even though we had the fish with Magnus, I'm already hungry. I think of the peanut butter and bread and granola bars and oranges. I know I could down it all in minutes. But I know I can't. I have to hold off. Don't even touch the water. Not yet.

I lean forward and pull my duffel bag out from beneath the foredeck. The food isn't soaked. Is that a good sign? Why did I ever think I could save Pogo by sailing away?

I look up and see only grayness. If the tide takes us one way, will it bring us back when it changes and flows the other way?

Where would that get us? We could be caught forever, pushed one way for six hours, then brought back again right where we started. We could spin in a tightening coil one way, then uncoil with the current and tide in the other direction. Out here, the coiling and uncoiling could be endless. But the fog can't last forever. Can it?

The fog looks denser than it did before. Beads of moisture line the cuffs of my sweatshirt. I can see them on Pogo's whiskers, too.

The light is dimming.

Do something about the sail.

I look down at my boat shoes. I could use the laces to stitch up the tear. But the laces might not be long enough or strong enough. I reach under the deck and bring out a length of line. If I unravel it, I can tie the thinner strands together to make a line long enough to do the job. I slice the bitter end off the line and unwind the three strands. I finish knotting them together to make a longer line, then drape the sail over my knees and with my jackknife set to coring holes in the Dacron sailcloth along the edge of the tear. Then I thread the strands through and tighten them. I knot off the line. Then I try to pull Pogo off the sail without waking him, but he lifts his head and looks at me.

"It's okay, boy." I slide him clear, and he gives me a look as if to say *Did you really have to do that? I was finally comfortable.*

At last I hoist the sail, then sit back in the cockpit and stroke Pogo's back.

The sail hangs as slack as before.

At least we're ready for the breeze—if the stitching holds. I work the tiller back and forth, making the water splash.

Waiting. Waiting is the worst. I can't do it. I have to choose a direction and paddle. If I paddle against the current, will we work our way back toward shore? I have to try. I sit up and grab the paddle and stab it into the water over the starboard side. The boat drives forward. The disk of water I can see around us seems to move with us—as if the boat isn't moving at all.

After three strokes, I move to the port side. I take three more strokes, then hobble on my knees back to the starboard side. My knees began to throb from kneeling and rocking on the hard deck.

Pogo lifts his head and gazes after me as I move from side to side.

I take three, four, five strokes. I know paddling on one side too long sends us off course, but I don't want to shift because kneeling sends pain sparking through my knees. I stop, chest heaving, and sit down hard on the deck. My knees throb.

The sound of water splashing comes to me through the fog.

I grip the paddle, trying to calm the sound of my breathing rushing in my ears. I hear more splashes, and a shriek pierces the fog. I stop breathing.

Another shriek reaches me, and then another and more after that, until I am surrounded by splashes and shrieks that echo in the fog.

Two shadows drop past me just as the water beside me erupts.

I look over the side and see a school of silvery, slender fish thrashing and leaping on the surface.

The shadows rise into the fog and vanish.

More geysers erupt beside me with a sound like someone doing cannonballs into the water. I hear other explosions of water beyond the wall of fog. We have drifted into the middle of a school of sand eels, and the gannets and gulls are in a feeding frenzy, dive-bombing them.

A bird with a wingspan as wide as my boat angles toward us.

It is a gannet—black and white wings, black mask, butterscotch neck and dagger beak—dropping out of the fog toward *Scallop*. I slide down onto the deck. It can't see the boat, hurtling down through the fog. It hits the water so hard and so close that spray douses us and flecks of fish diced by the razor-sharp bill flick into the cockpit.

Steve once told me that the birds sometimes go blind from years of plunging into the water, and that if they misjudge their dive, they could stun themselves—or break their necks.

Wincing, I kneel on the deck and lean over the starboard side to dig the paddle into the water, trying to steer away from the shrieks and cries and explosions of water around us.

They'll hit the mast if we don't get out of here. They'll tear the sail. They'll smash on the deck. The shadows circle. Another explosion showers us with seawater. Pogo shakes his head and sneezes.

Then from astern I hear slapping and splashing, and as I twist around to look, the scent of watermelon pours over me. I hear a sound like a wave breaking and then a splash. The striped bass are working the school of sand eels from below.

I paddle harder and harder to get out of the cauldron of birds and fish.

I wonder what Steve would do. He'd probably fish with the handline.

My arms weaken. The shrieks follow us as I jab the water with the paddle.

But I can't keep going like this.

Chapter Twelve

I paddle until my hands quiver so much I'm afraid I'll drop the paddle into the water. I sit back and slump to the deck, then stretch out on my back, staring up into the fog. I no longer hear the shrieking. The only sounds I hear are the slap and rattle of the sail and rigging and the gurgle of water as the boat rides over the surface.

A shadow slides over my face. Pogo is standing over me, looking down. He makes a small sound, a low hum.

"We're okay, boy." I reach up to scratch behind his silky ear. He tilts his head and leans his weight into my hand and closes his eyes. His lip droops.

"Thirsty?" Pogo looks at me. "Let's get a drink of water." I reach below the foredeck for the gallon jug and his canteen. I unscrew the lid and set the canteen down. Pogo goes to it and laps so fast half the water slops out of his mouth onto the deck. I tip up the jug and let the cold water gush into my mouth.

I have to force myself to lower the jug and count to ten to stop guzzling like Pogo.

Pogo's still at it, and I take hold of his harness and ease him away.

"That's enough for now. We've got to ration it."

I screw the lid back on and shove the canteen beneath the foredeck and then hold the jug for a moment and swish the water around in it. Thirst still scratches at me. I glance at Pogo, then raise the jug to my lips. *No!* I tell myself. *Do not.*

Do not drink. Not now. Not if you're not going to let Pogo drink more. I cap the jug and shove it under the deck.

I crawl back to the tiller and sit down, my back against the rail, then let myself slump till I am lying on my back. I stare up into the fog again. No one knows where we are and I don't know what to do.

My stomach knots and I feel the sting of tears in my eyes.

The fog darkens.

Now I feel the boat ride up a swell. I expect to feel us top the wave but the boat keeps rising. I sit up fast and grip the tiller. The boat sweeps upward, upward into the gloom as if riding an express elevator going up, until we finally slide down into the trough.

Where the big swell has come from puzzles me. The sea has been flat all day.

The boat lifts to the top of another swell, my stomach soaring with it as if I am riding to the top of a Ferris wheel. Then down we sled, down into the trough, the rigging rattling and slamming.

Pogo slides down the deck as we descend, then slides back the other way when we rise. He turns his head to me, confused.

In the trough I sheet the sail in tight to stop the boom from slashing back and forth, the block making a ringing clatter as I haul the line in.

Up again we rise.

I clamp my hands onto the tiller, trying to guide the boat as she rocks at the crest and then skims down the face of the swell. I know that if I don't keep her straight she could broach and capsize.

Some big storm must be blowing somewhere, causing the groundswell. I picture the colossal cloud coils of a hurricane.

Why did I want to sail far enough to see the wreck in the first place? Why didn't I just head home?

I hold on to the tiller, the rudder sending out a gargling wake as the boat descends.

I wanted to see the wreck. I wanted Pogo to see it, too. Then going back home would have been easier. But I wanted to see the wreck just like Steve had. I admit it: I was jealous.

The day after Steve and Dad got home from Malabar, Steve brought *Scallop* to the beach to clean her bottom—scrape off some of the barnacles and slime below her waterline. Pogo was lying on a towel nearby, snoring in the late afternoon sunshine.

"Too bad you missed the trip," Steve said. He was kneeling in the sand, his scraper grating against the skeg. "You would have loved it out there. You can see all the way to the abandoned lighthouse on the southern end and an old ruin on the northern tip that was a lookout tower in World War II. But the wreck was the best. We sailed out there, and you can hear the swells echo inside it."

The scraping stopped.

"So Sam." He stood up and squinted against the sun. He ran the back of his hand across his forehead. "Promise me something. I need you to take care of Pogo. He's a good old guy, the best around. He needs you. He's yours now. Remember that."

Two days later he was gone—with his Marine unit, deployed to Afghanistan.

Since then, Pogo had grown less and less interested in roaming the beaches and woods with me. Sure, he liked to sniff, but he couldn't walk far before he'd start limping.

Then one day that fall we found out about his tumor.

For a long time Pogo seemed fine. He just kept getting a little slower. He slept more and limped more. He grew more odd growths and lumps. Some mornings he only looked up at me from his bed. But other days he cantered around the yard.

One night he pooped in the house, and it began happening more and more. Each time, I saw glances pass between Mom and Dad. That went on all winter.

Then we got the news about Steve. We became a Gold Star

Family. The day was March 19. They told me when I came home from school. Mom did, I mean. She said—whispered, really—that it was from "wounds suffered when he encountered small-arms fire." Dad could only come down from his office and squeeze my shoulder and nod. Then he went back up. I didn't see him for a couple of days. I took Pogo and went down to the beach. The tide was low and a sharp wind was blowing and gulls hovered above the beach. The sun was so bright everything looked black and white. The waves made a sound like gasps. *Scallop* was still in winter storage and only the white plastic tube of the winter stick marked the mooring. I stared at the sparkles on the water. I wanted the dazzles to cut into my eyes like lasers and blind me. They started blurring and turning into prisms. I closed my eyes and sat down and Pogo nudged my armpit and I buried my face in his hot scruff.

Sitting here in the boat, my face again buried in Pogo's soft coat, I feel guilt twist my stomach.

I took Pogo away to save him. I admit I also wanted to see the things that Steve had seen. Really though, I just wanted to save Pogo. But out here among the building swells in thickening fog, the stab in my gut tells me all I've done is put him in more danger.

Chapter Thirteen

We reach the crest of the next swell. I hear a hiss like static somewhere ahead. Then we drop into the next trough, the wall of the swell ahead blocking off the sound. The boat rides up another wave and the sound is louder. The hiss spreads out across the fog before us.

I feel my skin squirm. We're headed into it.

I stand up in the cockpit to try to see through the fog. *Scallop* pitches forward off a crest, sending my feet out from under me as the boat skids sideways down the swell.

I grab for Pogo with one hand and the cockpit rail with the other, stopping us both from sliding forward. I scramble back to the tiller to bring the boat around just as another swell bulges up behind us.

Now the hiss has become a rushing roar—as if we are headed into the rapids of a raging river.

At the top of the swell I see patches of whiteness through the fog. A rip. We're being pulled into a rip. We can't make it through. I know it.

Where underwater shoals rose up from the deeps, tides and currents turn into acres of breaking seas. That's a rip. Fog Island Shoals is full of them—rips that have been swallowing ships for centuries.

The boat rises and I see a line of breakers just ahead of the bow, their crests stark white in the steel wool of the fog.

The first wave crashes onto the bow and cold green water

submerges the foredeck and bounds into the cockpit and pours a foot of numbing seawater around my legs.

I gasp, water dripping off my face.

The water catches Pogo and knocks him off his feet, lifting him up toward the rail as the water sloshes overboard. I grab his harness and pull him back to me.

The swell behind us catapults the boat into the waves. The bow rears up and the water pours out of the cockpit over the transom.

Down we go into the thick of the rip.

My ears fill with the thunder and roar of waves crashing over each other and surging up beside us.

A gray-green wall rises up before the boat and knocks her on her side. The water sloshes from the starboard deck to collide with water pouring in over the port rail.

I know I have to bail but I'm frozen at the tiller. If I let go for a moment, the boat will be swamped.

The stern tips up and the bow plows into the face of the oncoming wave. More green water courses over the boat and she shudders.

I spit out seawater. Pogo shakes and looks up at me, pleading with me to make the boat stop throwing us around. Maybe I should tie his harness to the boat. But if we capsize . . .

The boat shudders again as she is knocked backward. She spins around so that she heads stern-first into the next wave. Water gushes over the transom.

I fight to keep the tiller from flying out of my grip. The boat charges down, then shoots up, corkscrewing up the face of a wave. The rudder lashes the tiller back and forth. All I can do is hold on. Ahead I see more white patches.

"Don't let us go down," I cry. My voice is tinny amid the crash and explosion of the waves.

The boat shoots to the top of a wave and trips, heeling hard as the foaming crest thrusts at the hull. Gravity pulls me as the boat lifts and begins going over. I reach out to Pogo as

I slide on the tilting deck. I haul the tiller over and the boat comes around and shakes herself upright.

We shoot upward again, this time over a wave less steep than the others.

I squint ahead. I see only the fog, and that gives me a flicker of hope. There are see no more white patches, no more boiling breakers.

The boat settles into a trough and rocks for a moment before heading up again.

The noise now lies behind us. The field of breakers sounds like an immense sheet of foil being shaken and crushed and torn. The motion of the boat eases. I relax my grip on the tiller, my fingers stiff, my hands quivering.

"We're through it, Pogo. We made it." Holding the tiller in one hand, I reach for the bailer and scoop the water out of the cockpit. As I bail, my trembling calms.

But my stomach begs for food.

I stow the bailer and pull out the duffel. Hooking my arm around the tiller, I grab the bread and peanut butter. Pogo cocks his ears and tilts his head. "I'm just making a quick sandwich," I tell him. "Have to be careful with our supplies. We'll split it."

I pull out my jackknife and scoop out a wad of peanut butter and slather it on a slice of bread. Then I close another piece of bread over it. I bite into it and the salty sweet gumminess fills my mouth. Pogo's tail thumps on the deck.

I try to slow down, to chew in slow motion. In seconds half the sandwich is gone.

"Here you go." I tear off a piece of the remaining half and hold it out to Pogo. He stretches toward it, then takes it with his soft lips. It is gone in a moment, and he stares with hope at the rest, drooling.

What will I eat when we get home?

Peanut butter and Fluff—a fluffernutter sandwich on white bread. Two of them.

Blueberry pancakes with maple syrup. The roasted chicken with potatoes Mom makes now and then on Sundays. A lobster roll. A KitKat bar. Two fried eggs sunny-side up with toast that I can dip in the gooey yellow-gold yolks. Home fries and bacon.

And I'll let Pogo lick the plate.

I hand the rest of the sandwich to Pogo. With a click of his teeth it's gone.

I take a swig of water.

We will have to get more food if we're out here much longer. Food and water.

"People can last a long time without food," Steve told me once. "Water, not so much."

Then I feel it.

A puff of air slides around us, cool as fur.

The boom swings over to greet it.

Chapter Fourteen

The boat slips forward.

My heart jumps, and I see the sail belling out, small flutters rippling along the leech, telltales lifting like antennae searching for the breeze. I hear the wake gurgle and feel the resistance of the rudder in the quiver of the tiller.

"Look, Pogo. A breeze. A breeze at last."

He lifts his snout and searches the air for a scent.

I remember what Steve told me when I first started sailing: "When you're running before the wind, you want to ease off that throat halyard and lift the board a bit. She'll run better for you. Slack off before the wind."

I loosen the sheet, the boom swinging farther out. Then I lean forward and lift the centerboard partway up and cleat it off.

Will my stitch job hold?

The boat responds by leveling off and gaining speed, skimming over the wavelets. I strain to see ahead, but the fog thickens.

We are running blind, but just moving ahead is a kind of escape. Where we are escaping to, I'm not sure. What we're escaping from, I'm not sure, either. We could be heading in the direction of home. We could be heading north, toward Nova Scotia. We could be heading south, toward Bermuda or the Sargasso Sea.

We could be heading out to sea, beyond Fog Island Shoals, to the Gulf Stream, out to the ocean that is miles deep above the continental shelf and undersea canyons and the abyssal plain.

We could be heading across the Atlantic, and end up on the rocks off the coast of Ireland.

We are blind, a sightless gannet still diving after fish.

I have no GPS, no compass, no watch. All I have is a breeze that pushes us ahead, ahead toward somewhere.

The boat feels eager to go. She heels at a gentle angle, rising and dipping over the swells, the wavelets clucking against the hull.

I sit back, the tiller in my grip, the sail thrumming. Pogo circles once, twice, three times, then thumps down and curls up by me on the deck.

I'm overtaken by a sensation, a memory of hurtling on a bicycle downhill fast—at night with no lights, a summer night, Steve and me bicycling on Fog Island down a steep hill, Steve ahead, yelling "No hands!" a ghost image in the darkness, me following, my speed increasing, not letting go of the handles at first, the moist wind rushing past, the road black. Then a firefly flashed by.

I released the handles and stretched my arms wide, the bike and my heart racing faster.

Two more fireflies streaked by as I balanced, the wind in my face, until I felt the bike begin to wobble. I grabbed for the handles, the front tire scraping on the sand along the road as I wrestled the bike back on course. Swooping at last to level ground in a pool of light cast by a streetlamp, I coasted up beside Steve.

"No hands?" I said, trying to catch my breath.

My brother laughed. "Are you kidding? You could get killed that way."

The darkness thickens and the breeze decreases.

Soon the boat grows heavier and slows. The creak and hum of the rigging and the sail become a slapping.

Every time I blink, it seems, the light is dimmer.

The flashlight in the ditty bag—are the batteries dead? As the darkness closes in and the boat slows, I have to find out.

I leave the tiller, and fish under the foredeck for the bag. I paw inside it. At last I clutch the flashlight. "Here goes," I say to Pogo. A weak yellow light appears in the lens. In a moment it begins to fade. When I shake it, it brightens for a moment, then falters. I switch it off. It will not last more than a few minutes if I need to use it.

I hear a sound ahead that shoots fear into me, then a rush of hope; the sound of water washing against something solid.

Is that a boat? Could it be land? It can't be land.

I stand up and peer ahead. Through the fog, I make out a massive shadow darker than the dusky vapor around us.

Are we heading right for it, or is it heading right for us?

Chapter Fifteen

The shadow looms closer.

I hear the wash of a wave, and I peer into the fog.

The shadow is not moving.

I bring the boat around, the sail flagging, to point the bow right at the shadow. The closer we get, the larger the shadow grows.

I grab the paddle and stroke the boat ahead. I can feel my mouth drop open as an immense rock formation rises out of the fog. My mind stumbles as I struggle to place what I am seeing. How can a massive rock formation materialize out of nowhere?

But it is no rock formation.

The vast hull of a ship, its bow slanted upward into the fog, takes shape, towering above me. I hear another wave wash against the vessel, and the echo and rumble of the wave within the hull.

"The wreck!" I back-paddle to keep the boat from driving against the hull. "It's the wreck, Pogo."

The ship's forward section juts up at a forty-five degree angle. I can just make out the flare of the bow high above me in the fog. Below the rail I see the name of the ship, the paint on the lettering chipped and rust-stained: RAEBURN.

This is the wreck Dad and Steve sailed around last summer. The wreck. The wreck is about ten miles off Malabar Island. My heart surges.

If we can stay here, in the morning I'll know where we

are. If I drift around all night in the fog, we could end up anywhere.

I throw the paddle down and dive beneath the foredeck to pull out a coil of line.

Pogo jumps up and wags his tail.

"Stay," I tell him. "I mean it. Stay."

Then I worm my way up the foredeck to the prow to make the line fast to the bow cleat. Must be somewhere to tie up to it, I think, peering at the hull. My heart hammers. I can't let us drift away.

Already the remaining light is seeping into darkness.

I try to fix my eyes on the hulk beside us. I jump back into the cockpit and grab the paddle. I take a couple of strokes to get us close enough to glimpse the swell riding up the side of the rusted hull. The swells are too high here. Maybe around the other side.

I paddle toward the port side, swinging the boat beneath the bow section of the ship, the shadow of it plunging us into darkness. The splashes of the paddle echo beneath the hull.

When we come around to the other side, the water calms, the bulk of the ship blocking the current. I bring the boat along the hull to where the rail meets the sea and see a bent stanchion thrusting up from the water. I take two hard strokes to drive the boat toward the hull, then leap to the foredeck as we drift closer. I pluck up the coiled line, hold on to the forestay and lean over to grab the stanchion before the boat hits the hull. My hands quivering, I throw a hitch around the stanchion and then grab the cold, slick steel of the wreck's rail.

A burst of air blasts my face and the churning of large wings surrounds me. I crouch down. My hand slips but I get a hold again before the boat drifts off.

The wingbeats vanish into the darkness. Birds. Big ones.

The boat rises on the swell. We could stay aboard or climb onto the wreck to find more shelter. Either way, we're staying put for the night.

The thought of wedging together below *Scallop*'s foredeck till first light sends a shiver through me. I could drape the cockpit cover over the brace and fasten it around the coaming to form a small tent. But if we need to sail away fast, the cover could get in the way.

I picture Pogo and me, the two of us shivering all night as the boat rides off the wreck, shrouded in fog. Better try to get aboard while a little light's left.

I let go of the rail and the boat slips away with the current. The line goes taut, snubbing her, and she swings around to ride away from the hull, the current running hard enough to bubble behind her rudder.

Better heave to, the way Steve showed me, so I can leave the sail up in case I have to shove off fast. I find a short length of line beneath the foredeck, sheet the sail in tight and lash the tiller hard to windward with the line.

Now she'll always come up into the wind.

I dig beneath the foredeck for the cockpit cover, a vinyl-coated canvas tarp, fold it, take the flashlight and crawl back on top of the foredeck.

Hand over hand I pull on the line to bring the boat back to the wreck. I tuck the cover under my arm and shove the flashlight into my pocket.

A low hum comes from Pogo.

"You wait here." I try to keep my voice steady. "I need to go check out the wreck. You wait till I get back."

He makes the hum again and tucks his tail, its tip twitching.

"You're a good boy. I'll be back."

I wait for the swell to raise the boat, then say "Now" out loud and reach for the stanchion and swing myself onto the sloping steel plates of the deck. As I hit, my feet fly out from underneath me and I land on the flashlight in my pocket. Pain shoots streaks of light into my eyes.

Reaching for a better grip, I feel the cover slide out from

under my arm and slip past my leg. I pin it to the deck with the toe of my boat shoe.

Wings batter the darkness around my head, and I strain to keep myself from slipping into the water while I press my foot against the cover. The flapping circles me as I drag the cover closer with my foot till I can grab it. I clamp it under my arm and feel around until my foot rests on another stanchion. I put my weight on it and reach into my pocket for the flashlight. When I switch it on, the feeble beam sends a dim cone of light into the fog. A black form flaps through it, and I catch a momentary glimpse of a red eye.

Cormorant. They must roost here.

In the thin beam I spot a hatchway in the middle of the deck. I shut off the flashlight and pocket it. Then I swing my right leg out onto the deck and get a grip with my foot on the steel plating slick with salt and bird guano.

I move like a crab, sideways, the cover locked beneath my arm. The surface is rough with rust in spots, slick in others. A few slabs crumble like crackers underfoot. The deck angles like a low-pitched roof.

I reach the edge of the hatchway and hold onto the lip. I haul myself onto the ledge and sit for a moment to catch my breath. As my breathing calms, the shivers return and my teeth chatter.

The swells rise and fall around the hull, sloshing and washing.

I switch the flashlight back on. The beam quivers as I play it inside the hatchway. I spot a set of metal stairs tipped like a ramp toward a floor.

I turn off the flashlight and pull myself onto the stairs, feeling my way down into the black well. The metal walls echo with the sound of the water within the ship's hull as if I've entered an undersea grotto. I feel for the floor and reach out to touch the slick wall. The wall and floor form a vee.

We can sit down here. It'll be better shelter for Pogo than staying on *Scallop*.

I flick on the flashlight and stagger backward, my breathing frozen at the sight: The beam points through a doorway opening onto green seawater sloshing inside the hull five feet below, a two-foot bulkhead all that stands between the water and me.

I could have fallen down there. I could have fallen into the water. I'll have to keep a close eye on Pogo.

I edge to the side, the flashlight fading to a hint of lemon. I switch it off. Blackness swallows me. I leave the cockpit cover on the floor and feel my way back up the ladder onto the deck, then ease myself down the slope to where I tied up *Scallop*. I pull the line to bring *Scallop* up to the rail. I switch on the flashlight again, about to call Pogo, and what I see in the yellow beam makes me freeze.

"Don't, Pogo, no!" I call. "Stay."

He's on the foredeck, right at the bow, teetering on the edge. I can hear his humming over the sound of the swells washing against the wreck.

"Don't move!" I yell, panic rising inside me. I keep pulling the boat toward me. I see him rock forward, losing his balance. I'm pulling too fast.

I have to slow down. "Easy, boy. Don't move."

The moment the bow of the boat nudges the hull, Pogo scrambles and leaps, his claws scraping the deck and clattering on the steel. I grab his harness and pull but I hear a deep splash and his weight pulls me down toward the water. My foot hooks onto the stanchion and he's struggling but I have him. I heave upward and fling him onto the rusty deck and clamp my arms around him.

He tries to worm away at first but then he's licking my cheek and my nose and my ears and he's tickling me. "You're crazy," I say, laughing. "You think I'd leave you behind?"

I guide him down the steps of the ladder into the compartment. He presses his nose against the floor, then sniffs the walls.

"Don't go wandering over here." I point the flashlight at the open doorway and let him sniff the bulkhead. "Nothing but water below."

I unfold the cockpit cover. "Okay, boy. Let's get under this." I wrap it around me, then lower myself to the sloping floor. The steel feels clammy.

"Come over here. We'll be warmer."

He steps over to me, and I reach up and wrap the cover around us both.

"Okay, lie down." I have to force him down because otherwise he'll turn circles and we'll never stay covered. At first he resists but then he lies down beside me. I feel his breathing and smell his warm loaf-of-bread smell. "That's good." I switch off the flashlight. "That's a good boy."

From deep within the hull I hear creaks and groans, water sloshing and metal grating. I hope nothing else is down here with us.

A larger swell sweeps through the cavity below, and the ship itself sways and shudders. The air smells of fish and seaweed and rust and salt.

I hear the rustle of wings above the hatchway.

My shivers come in waves even though Pogo's warm beside me.

Get us through the night, I say to myself, blinking my eyes in the blackness, trying to make my muscles unclench.

Just get us through.

Chapter Sixteen

I jolt awake.

I'm wedged in the trough made by the wall and floor. The wreck is swaying. I fling my arms out, banging my elbow against the metal, to try to thrust the cover off me.

Pogo is gone!

"Pogo!"

For a moment when the swell pours in below, a pale green light comes through the doorway. I struggle up and shuck the cover off. I hear the low hum. Pogo is standing at the doorway, looking over the bulkhead.

I grab hold of his harness and peer down into the water. The wave that washes in flickers with phosphorescence. Below the surface I see a massive submarine-shaped form slip into view, glide around in a circle, hover for a moment, then speed out of sight, leaving a trail of green-white light.

I take a step back, pulling Pogo with me, then lose my balance and sit down hard on the slanted floor.

I can't believe what I've seen. A shiver of dread runs over the back of my neck.

That was the biggest shark ever!

When I look up through the hatchway, I see two bright stars swimming through a pool of clear sky between fog puffs.

I tell Pogo to stay put and I scramble up the steps. I have to find the Big Dipper.

I hear my brother saying, "Just draw an imaginary line from the bottom two stars in the bowl of the constellation. That'll lead you to Polaris, the North Star. Then you can fix your position." If I can find it and take a bearing with a point on the ship, tomorrow I will know which direction to head, even with Malabar Island out of sight over the horizon.

I scan the sky. Already puffs of fog squeeze over the two stars. Another star appears in a slice of open sky. But it is only one, and before I can make out what it is, the fog locks it out of sight.

Where's *Scallop*?

I look over the side of the wreck. The boat is not there. My breathing stops. Then I look farther forward. The pale triangular shape of the sail appears just off the hull. She must have swung forward in the current.

"You'll be fine," I say out loud. I wonder if I mean *Scallop* or myself.

Heaving-to allows the boat to ride out almost any wind that might come up. She will swing in long arcs, falling off, then coming back up into the wind. She'll be ready if anything happens. She's okay. I'm sure of it. I'll have to check her as soon as it's light.

I feel my way back down the steps into the compartment.

"Everything's okay, boy." I pat Pogo on the head and peer through the doorway. Water sloshes through. The hull creaks and trembles.

I've got to get some rest. Tomorrow I have to be ready.

I sit down and gather Pogo to me and wrap the cover around us. I settle us into the vee and stare up at the opening above. The fog has folded over the stars and now the hatchway is dark. My stomach grinds with hunger pangs.

I should have brought some supplies from the boat, but I

just have to stop thinking about it till daylight. It's too risky to try to get back aboard now.

I picture the form of the creature swimming—the shark, if that's what it was. It looked to be at least as long as my boat.

I wish I'd brought the water, and the more I think about the water, the thirstier I get.

Go to sleep, I tell myself. *Get some rest*. My stomach groans and my tongue feels thick with dryness.

A wave washes in below, echoing as it breaks, and the ship sways, the metal groaning.

I think of a glass of water, of holding a clear glass below the faucet and letting it fill till it spills over, bubbling down with a rushing sound, and then I put the glass to my mouth and drink, and drink, and drink, the water flowing out of the faucet with the silkiest, coolest, most refreshing sound ever.

What did Steve say? "You can last without food for a long time. Water, not so much."

My stomach twists. I have to stop thinking about it. I turn my thoughts to morning instead.

The sun will be out. I will be able to see again. Seeing.

Has anyone started looking for us yet?

I reach over and find Pogo's head, and stroke his velvety buckskin ears. They are curled like potato chips. He must know something is wrong.

A new sound comes to me, something I haven't heard over the thudding of my heart and the creaks and groans of the wreck and the wash of the water.

I hear a sound like breathing coming through the metal of the deck, coming from above.

Chapter Seventeen

As I listen, the breathing stops. The wash of the waves and the groan of the metal are all I can hear.

Don't go up there, I tell myself. *Not yet. Wait till daylight. It might be nothing.*

I try to keep my attention focused. The harder I listen, the more I feel exhaustion weigh me down. But I do not want to fall asleep.

The sound comes again, yanking me back from the brink of sleep.

Ghosts. The ghosts of the crew that went down with the ship are moving on deck. Maybe we should climb back aboard *Scallop* and stay under the foredeck till dawn. I do not want to face ghosts.

Have Mom and Dad called the Coast Guard yet?

The breathing sounds reach me again, closer now. I sit up, my heart stuttering.

It's coming for us.

I wait, looking up at the patch of blackness in the hatchway. I hear my heart churning in my ears, so loud I'm sure whatever is out there can hear it, too. I strain to catch the next sound. Maybe I should go take a look. I keep listening. I can't make myself move. Pogo is sitting up beside me, listening too.

What kind of men were lost on this ship? Are their ghosts still here? Is someone on deck—one of the ghosts? More than one? Swaying with the ship? Are they down here with us?

I realize, as I wait for the next sound, that at least I'm not thinking about being hungry or thirsty or how I made a mistake by trying to rescue Pogo in the first place.

How long we sit there, I don't know. I begin to count the waves washing in: twenty-nine, thirty, forty-two . . . I finally stretch out on my back and Pogo lies on his side and I pull the cover over us.

Stay awake, I tell myself, my eyes closing. *You have to stay awake.*

Wave after wave washes in, the ship swaying with them.

The distant rustling in my ears is the last sound I remember.

I wake with a start. The hatchway is only a paler rectangle of black. I wonder how long we've been down here. Daybreak has to be arriving soon.

I listen to the water gulp and exhale, and I try to count the seconds, wishing we could climb back into the boat, wishing we were sailing home, wishing I had a cheeseburger in one hand and a chocolate frappe in the other, wishing, wishing most of all that Steve was here with us.

But when I think of sailing home, dread hits me for what Pogo will be facing when we get there. I picture us crossing the beach, and then we dissolve into blackness. I rest my head against Pogo's shoulder and listen to the sounds of the ship.

I blink. The rumpled white material of the cockpit cover is glistening in dusty light. Pogo's snout sticks out from underneath as he snores his soft snuffle.

Above me, an oblong moon pulls free of the passing shreds of fog to cast light down on us. Flecks of fog fly past. A dark shape moves into view across the hatchway. My skin creeps. The shape spreads out, looking like a fin or a long-necked beast. Is it going to drop down on top of us?

I scramble out of the cover and charge up the ladder. I hear a rustling, then the flap of wings as I reach the top.

The shape vanishes. The slanted deck is washed in moonlight, and now I see my ghosts, my fin, my long-necked beast. Cormorants line the upswept rail in single file. Some hold their wings spread-eagled. Some take off and beat away in the moonlight. Others huddle up the rail away from me.

I draw my arm across my mouth and shake my head. Stupid. I'm so stupid. I should have known.

Steve would have cracked up about it. "Spooked by cormorants," he'd say. "What a riot."

I sit on the frame of the hatchway, watching the clumps of fog slip past the moon. From below I hear Pogo hum. "I'll be right back," I call. "Don't be scared."

What part of the sky was the moon in the last time I saw it? If I knew, I could get my bearings and know which way to sail in the morning—if the fog lifts.

Now and then the fog parts enough so I can see the moonlight on the crawling skin of the sea, the deck thrust into the air toward the moon.

The cormorants stand along the rail in silhouette.

I turn to look down at *Scallop*.

A cormorant flaps away as I realize the boat is gone.

Chapter Eighteen

"No!" My voice echoes in the hollows of the ship. "No!"

My cries spook the birds closest to me off the rail. The ones farther up the bow edge away, crowding tighter together and making low grunts as they peer about in the moonlight.

I slide over to where I tied the boat to the ship. Fog slithers across the moon and blots it out. I pull the flashlight out of my pocket, shake it and switch it on. Nothing. The flashlight is dead.

The moon comes back out. In its blue-tinged light, I look at the stanchion. Why? Why did the boat drift away? How did the knot come loose? Should I have dropped the sail? Should I have stayed aboard?

I crawl back to the hatchway. We're going to die out here. I tried to save Pogo but now I'm the one who'll make him die.

No food. No water. No boat.

I hear the birds rustling, then wings flapping as the ones I spooked return to roost.

The moon winks, then the lid of fog closes over it.

Hot tears cool on my cheeks in the cold vapor.

I climb down the ladder, my knees weak, my hands quivering. I pat the floor for the cover, find it, reach out for Pogo and wrap us up again. "Now I've really done it," I say in a low voice.

A wave rolls in. The hulk sways.

When morning comes, someone'll come looking for us. Someone is looking for us. Someone has to be.

I must have slipped into a deep sleep because when I flick my eyes open, blackness fills them and the air has chilled. Shivers come over me in waves. From somewhere, I hear dripping. Dripping. Water. I lick my cracked lips. Maybe it's fresh water. I sit up and run my tongue around my mouth, the roof as dry as sand. The drips seem to be coming from close by.

I strip off the cover and get on my hands and knees. Pogo struggles upright and noses me. The metal surface feels cold and moist and rough with rust.

"Help me find the water, boy."

I pat the floor before me and move forward. I stop to listen. The drips seem closer.

Reaching out, I brush my hand against a wall. It's wet. I touch my fingers to the wetness, then bring them to my mouth.

It's fresh water. Maybe it's the fog, condensing on deck, then seeping through the porous hull. But where are the drips?

I get up on my knees and reach up the wall. A drop rolls down my finger and I suck at it as if it were a lollipop. The dripping is nearby. I run my hand along the ceiling of the compartment. There. I feel a drip plop onto my palm.

I press my shoulder against the wall and tip up my face. A drop splashes on my forehead. I tip my head back farther. The next drop taps my lip. A little to the left. Pogo pushes up beside me, nudging me off balance.

"Hang on. I've almost got it."

The next drop hits my tongue. I swirl it in my papery mouth. But I can't get enough this way. I have to figure out something else. I feel in my pocket. The flashlight. I yank it out and unscrew the lens holder. It can work as a cup. I hold it up toward the drip.

Plink. Splat. Plink.

I steady my arm with my other hand. The drips splash into the cup. How long will I have to hold this? My arm begins quivering. I grab my wrist with my other hand to support it.

Just a little longer.

Plop. Splash. Plop.

I clench my stomach to keep myself from dropping my arms as the drips splash into the cup. A little more. Just hold it up. At last I sit down on the floor and lift the cup to my mouth.

I set the rim against my lips, holding the cup with both hands, and tip it. Cool liquid slides over my tongue and then evaporates. I taste rust.

Then I hear Pogo hum, and his toenails scratch on the floor. I tip the cup farther up, then stop.

He needs the water more than I do. I reach out and pull him toward me.

"There's just a couple of drops in here," I say. "Give me your snout."

I guide his nose toward the cup and he sniffs and slurps and laps. I can hear his tongue swirl against the empty cup.

"At least it was something. Right?"

I put my hand back and feel the drips flick against my palm. I put the cup beneath the drips and lower it till it rests between the slanting floor and the wall.

"We'll just leave it there. In a while we'll have more to drink."

I shuffle back, pulling Pogo with me, and draw the cover around us. I listen to the drips, counting them as they hit the cup. At one hundred thirty-seven I drift off to sleep, still sunk in blackness, my dog breathing beside me, the ship breathing around us.

Chapter Nineteen

I wake up from a dream of sitting in front of the woodstove in Magnus's place, Pogo resting his grizzled chin on my knees. My back and shoulder, close to the fire, were so hot they became itchy.

I blink. A beam of sunshine lances through a crack in the ship's hull, warming my shoulder and lighting the compartment.

Pogo is snoring, his head in my lap.

I look up through the hatchway and see blue sky.

I blink again. A shape moves into the rectangle—a long hooked beak, a slender black head, an arched neck, a staring eye. A cormorant. It looks down at me, tilting its head one way, then the other.

I do not move. What does the bird want?

It hops up on the rim of the hatchway and cranes its neck down, looking from Pogo to me, inspecting us. Maybe it thinks we're hurt. Maybe it wants to eat me. But do cormorants eat dead things? I thought they only ate fish.

I blink. The cormorant blinks.

"Hi, bird. You looking for something?"

The cormorant turns its head. I see that its left eye socket is an empty, blackened cavity. Then it tips its beak up and flares its wings, holding them out as if it is about to fly. It bends its neck around to preen its breast feathers. It flaps its wings, shakes its beak back and forth and wags its tail. Then it peers down at me for a moment before stepping backward and disappearing.

I ease the cover off, trying not to wake Pogo, and turn to find the cap of the flashlight.

It's full.

I lift it and sip the water, trying not to guzzle it. I have to save some for Pogo. He looks up and yawns. "Here you go." I cradle his head and he touches his nose to the cup, going cross-eyed the way he used to when he did the trick with the treat, and then slurps the rest of the water.

"That's it for now." I set the empty cup below the drip again.

"Want to go topside?" I say. "It's sunny out."

He hauls himself up and I take hold of his harness and lead him up the ladder. At the top I wince, blinded by the brilliant light. I hold one arm out to shield my eyes. Scraps of fog lie close to the water surface, tinged pink in the early light. So that's east. I look across the water toward the sun. Now I know that the bow of the wreck, facing west, is pointing toward home.

I look along the rail at the cormorants lining it and wonder which one was watching us through the hatchway. I count eleven birds. Some hold their wings open to dry in the sun.

I run my eyes along the length of the mast slanting overhead. I didn't see it before, hidden as it was in the dark and the fog. It is thick as a telephone pole and coated in chalky cormorant guano.

At the tip of the mast perches a cormorant. It flaps its wings but does not fly. Is that the one? It turns its head to look at me.

Just then my stomach lets out a long series of creaks. No dinner. No breakfast. Nothing to eat. I've never been this hungry before.

I look at Pogo. Think how he must feel.

I look at the birds again. Maybe eating one of them is the answer. How fast would I have to be to grab one? How would I cook it? The thought of eating raw bird makes my stomach roll.

I think of the handline back aboard the boat. I could catch our own fish if I had it. If I had our boat, we'd be on our way home. Where the currents and tides are now taking the boat, I cannot guess. The tide itself, turning during the night, might have somehow twisted the boat back on the line and pulled it free. Maybe I just tied a bad knot. Maybe it just loosened up and let go. Where will the wind and currents take her?

I hear a splash from the water below. A seal hauls itself out onto the sloping deck, the surge of a swell washing around it. It glistens in the light, its dark fur slick and glossy. It looks up at me with wide eyes. Pogo bristles and cocks his ears and hums. I grab for his harness as the seal hunches away to dive beneath the surface.

I wouldn't have done anything to it. Its eyes looked like Pogo's.

I watch the surface. The seal does not reappear. I let the sun toast my face. The blue of the sea, the pearl and pink and gray of the fog puffs, the powder-blue sky . . . we are no closer to home, but we can see. At last we can see.

From the direction the seal went I hear a faint drone. From out there, beyond the scattered clumps of fog, comes the mumble of a ship's engine.

I scan the water. All I can see are the clumps of broken fog, the brilliant sun and sunlight shattering on the surface.

The wreck groans as a swell rolls in. The sound of the vessel's engine grows closer. I keep sweeping my eyes along the horizon in the direction of the sound, my heart whirring. There, to the east of the wreck, a vessel with a fire-engine-red hull steams out of a clump of fog, on a course for the wreck.

My heart dances. I have to find a way to signal the boat.

I can see her approaching, her high prow and pilothouse windows winking in the sunlight and her radar on the pilot-house roof twirling. She is a dragger, a fishing vessel about a hundred feet long. Soon she is close enough that I can read the name beneath the bow rail: MISS FORTUNE.

I've seen that boat before. Her home port is Fog Island itself. We passed her at the town dock on our way toward Fog

Island Light and open water. We could hitch a ride right back to the wharf.

When we passed her, her red hull was vivid in the morning sunshine as she took on supplies for a trip. Now the same red boat is heading straight for us.

I leap up and wave my arms. "Here! Over here!"

Wait. I need a better way. I peer down through the hatchway. The cover.

Chapter Twenty

I scramble down the ladder and snatch up the cover.

Miss Fortune is changing course as she nears the wreck, swinging her port side to us. I see the cables angling into the water from the drum on the stern work deck, the wake bubbling and churning as the vessel tows her net along the sea floor.

One chance. This is it.

I hear the rumble of the engine, and now the wash and gurgle of the wake. No one is on deck.

The vessel rolls in the smooth swells.

They'll never see me. I'm down too low.

I look up at the mast rising over my head and run my eyes out to its tip. The cormorant looks back at me and flaps its wings. I've got to get out there.

"You stay, Pogo. I'll be right back. You stay, hear me?"

Pogo droops his ears and makes his humming sound.

"Good boy."

Clamping the cover under my arm, I crawl up the slanting deck toward the base of the mast, moving as fast as I can, knowing if I push too hard I'll slip.

The cormorants along the rail edge away from me as I climb.

I glance at the vessel: Now she is about half a football field off, still on a heading that will bring her close by.

I reach the base of the mast and hoist myself up onto it. I sling my legs over the sides.

Straddling it, I hitch my way out toward the end.

From the dragger's exhaust stack, a plume of black smoke pours out as she throttles up. I hear the engine growl.

I have to hurry. The faster I go, the more I risk losing my balance, and I have fight to keep from slipping. I glance at the vessel, then turn back to look up at the mast extending out into the air, the sunlight in my eyes.

I look down. The deck slopes into the water, the bulge of a swell running up it to within a few feet of the hatchway and the compartment where we spent the night. Pogo looks up at me, wagging his tail.

My hands go wobbly.

Farther out. I have to go farther.

The dragger lolls over the swells, rising and falling and rolling as she comes closer, now within twenty-five yards of the wreck.

When I look down again, I am high above the water. Sunlight squiggles in the depths. The cormorant remains at the tip. It looks at me and flaps its wings.

The vessel wallows closer, her engine making a rapid, rattling *thud-thud-thud* across the water. Now I can see the entire length of the hull, rust streaks staining the side from her scuppers and a stream of water pumping out from a black hose draped over her rail. I see a figure move behind the pilot-house windows.

"Now!" I gasp, and I yank the cover from under my arm.

I shake it open and wave it over my head, shaking it back and forth, yelling "Hey! Hey! Over here!"

The vessel pushes onward, her bow wake curling white not fifteen yards off the wreck. I yell so loud my voice squeaks. I wave the cover, reaching as high as I can, and I feel the strength in my arms ebbing away.

Anger shoots through me. "You idiots! Over here!"

I know I am slipping as it happens but I can't do anything to stop myself. I have no grip on the round surface. I can't shift my weight. Gravity takes hold of me.

I spin around the mast, my legs still clenching it like a wrench stripping a bolt, until I am upside down, hanging by my legs, my strength failing, gravity gaining. I see the cormorant watching me from upside down just before I drop.

I have only a moment to inhale before I hit the water and the air is being crushed out of me by the shock of the cold. Submerged, I hear the whir of *Miss Fortune*'s propeller. I kick hard, my right fist still clenched onto the cockpit cover.

Don't let go of it. Don't try to breathe.

I grope with my left hand, kick again and break through into the air. Already the current is taking me away from the wreck.

I frog-kick and breast-stroke, the cover wrapping itself around my right arm.

From water level, the mass of the wreck blocks my view of the dragger.

Then, below me, I see the shadow—the shadow that is as big as my boat, the one I saw in the phosphorescence. I go rigid.

The shadow passes below me, slows, then dissolves into the depths beyond the wreck.

I launch myself through the icy water, driving against the current, my only thought to get to the wreck. I look up once, salt water pinching my eyes. I'm gaining on it. I don't dare look around to see if the shadow is coming back. A swell lifts me and I throw my arms forward to break my momentum as I slam onto the deck.

I scrabble for a stanchion, latch onto it, gasping, and turn onto my back to see a seal slip off the opposite side of the deck into the water.

I stay on my back, chest heaving, lungs seared. I hear Pogo's low humming, and I twist my head around to see him standing above me on the slanted deck, his tail revolving.

I crawl back up beside him, wrap an arm around him and look over the water.

The dragger is slipping into a clump of fog, her stern to us,

MISS FORTUNE, FOG ISLAND on the transom blurring as she disappears from view.

I look down. I still have hold of the cover. It drips salt water that runs down the deck in jagged streams. But my hat, my Pogo hat, is gone.

I look along the length of the mast. The one-eyed cormorant raises itself and flaps its wings.

Chapter Twenty-One

For a long time I cling to the stanchion. My chest rises and falls fast and hard at first, then begins to calm.

I listen to the sound of *Miss Fortune*'s engine diminishing until all I hear are waves washing around the wreck and Pogo humming.

What did I do wrong? I should have been ready to signal them earlier. I shouldn't have slipped. I shouldn't have panicked in the water. Steve told me never to flail if I saw a shark. Steve also told me about a shark that grabbed a seal when he and Dad were beachcombing on Malabar Island.

"It took that seal in a second, hitting from below," he said. "It was like a rocket had hit it. The seal didn't have time to make a sound, but the bite of the shark sounded like crunching lettuce."

At least I held on to the cover. But I'll never see that hat again.

The sun climbs. The wreck groans and sways. The cormorants take off to fish, flap back to the wreck, then take off to fish again.

The fog begins to break apart, shredding and then melting to reveal the open ocean stretching out around us. Gulls fly in the sky high above. Gannets flap by.

I scan the horizon. No boats. Nothing but waves.

If a boat appears, I need to be ready. I look up at the bow pointing high above us. I know I have to climb up there. If I can keep a lookout there, and a boat comes by, it is sure to see me. But I thought *Miss Fortune* would see me, too. Why didn't they see me?

The sun warms me up. The warmer I get, the more thirst grips me. Pogo pants beside me.

I lead Pogo down into the compartment. "You have to stay down here," I tell him. "I have to go to the bow, and I don't want you slipping overboard."

He hums and lowers his ears.

"We don't have any choice. You just get some rest, okay?" I pat him on the head and go back up.

I fold the cover and jam it in the waist of my pants so I can have two hands free. I climb along the rail, using the stanchions as handholds.

The cormorants grunt as they move away from me. They crowd together near the bow.

I stop to catch my breath, and turn to look at the mast. A cormorant—the one-eyed cormorant—roosts at the end. I look beyond the mast, far to the east. I can see a band of soot-gray vapor lying on the horizon, its top edge fringed with wisps. More fog.

I scan the horizon to the north. Nothing but the arc of the ocean appears.

Go to the top.

I pull in a breath and reach up for the next stanchion, and lever myself up. The stanchion pops and sends me sliding down the deck, skidding along the rusted plates and rivets, headed toward the water. I grab hold of another stanchion and slam to a stop.

"Stupid! Why am I so stupid?"

My right hand throbs. I pull myself up and look at my palm. It is scraped raw. I try to suck at it, but my mouth is so dry no saliva wets it.

At least the cover cushioned my fall.

Go to the top. Not far to go. Keep going. I push on, testing each stanchion to see if it will hold me before stepping up.

As I near the prow, the birds grunt and edge away, then flap off. At the top, I cling to the rail and draw in a deep breath.

I turn to look back at the broken mast. The one-eyed cormorant stands at the tip, flexing its wings. Then it lowers its head and swoops off to flap low over the water, its shadow tailing it on the surface below.

I run my eyes over the waves. From my new vantage point high above the sea, the waves are sun-splattered scales stretching to the horizon in every direction. I rotate, looking from east to north to west. Then I stop and squint. Is that a streak of land to the west? Can it be Malabar? Or is it only another clump of fog?

I stare out at it. The low puffs of fog spread farther apart toward the west, blanking out the streak from view. Looking out at the western horizon, at what must be Malabar Island, I clench the iron rim of the prow till my hands quake and a sob rises inside me like a fountain.

How could I be so close to land but not be able to get there? I lower my head and rest it on my forearm, and squeeze my eyes shut. With my eyes closed, I see only pinkish light from the sun.

I hear a cry from down on the wreck. It's Pogo, wailing. I have to go check on him. I have to. First I look up and squint at the western horizon, toward the fleck that might be land.

Another sound reaches me—a sound like a thin breaking wave, coming from the same direction.

Chapter Twenty-Two

The sound of the wave lingers.

I listen. I don't know what it is.

Pogo wails again, and I look down at the hatchway. "Hang on!" I call.

The sound becomes a throaty whoosh.

I peer harder into the glare. Something's out there, something's making that sound.

Why can't I see it?

I focus on the water leading up to the pencil stroke that is the island, seeing only the openness of the water, the waves rolling over the distance between the wreck and the island.

The sound is getting louder.

I could never swim to the island. How many miles is it? Ten? Eleven?

Steve told me once that even on the clearest of days the farthest you could see standing on the deck of a boat was thirteen miles, so that when you sailed, your world was a disk with a radius of thirteen miles.

But up here, on the bow, I am maybe fifty feet above sea level, and I can see farther.

The sound is the tearing rush of a jet aircraft.

A glint in the blue catches my eye, and I spot a plane heading our way from the direction of the island.

Pogo cries out again, and the cry pierces my gut. But I can't leave. Not now. Not when I might be able to save us.

"Hang on!" I shout. "A plane is coming."

At first it does not seem to be moving fast. It is still too far away to identify.

I brace myself against a stanchion and unfold the cover.

The plane flashes, its course straight into the sun. I hear the whistle of the engines as it begins to take shape. I loop my arm around the stanchion, my eyes locked on the airplane. Now I can see that it has a white fuselage and twin engines behind swept-back wings.

It sweeps toward us, banking one way, then the other.

I swallow. My heart jumps when I make out the angled orange band with a thin blue stripe behind the plane's nose.

Coast Guard.

"Hey!" I shout, just as Pogo cries again. The plane's engines scream as it approaches.

I raise the cover and slash it back and forth over my head. "Here! We're here!"

The engines screech louder as the plane grows in the sky. It comes on fast, heading dead for the wreck.

I lash the cover, my body beginning to shake, my eyes tracking the jet driving toward me, my voice and Pogo's cries drowned out as the engines rip the air with a shrieking roar that sends the cormorants leaping from the rail, scattering away above the water.

The plane shoots so close overhead I can read the US COAST GUARD painted on the underside of its left wing and the US insignia on the right wing and the number of the aircraft beneath the copilot's window: 2421.

As it passes, it sends a shock wave of roaring air down on me that makes me crouch and look away, clutching the cover to me. In seconds it is receding toward the east, banking, climbing, its shadow blinking over me and the wreck. I watch it become a speck in the northeast, then change course, dip and fly low over the water to the north.

The sounds of the waves washing against the wreck settle back around us. The one-eyed cormorant returns to land on the end of the mast. Folding the cover, I watch the bird as it opens its wings to the sun. It looks like some kind of angel. The sunlight catches in its feathers and they give off a dark iridescence.

Pogo is okay—scared, but okay. I climb back up the bow to go on watch again. He probably thought I had left him, that I wasn't coming back. But I cannot bring him up here with me or he might slip and fall. For now he's quiet.

The sun reaches the top of its arc.

I keep my eyes on a cloud sliding high above the water from the west, a small white one that curls like a breaking wave as it leads its shadow across the water.

The sun toasts my clothes and warms me up. I pull off my sweatshirt and tie it around my waist. I stay on watch, afraid that if I crawl into the compartment for even a moment with Pogo I might miss another chance at waving down a vessel or an aircraft.

Cormorants fly off to fish or return to preen and open their wings to dry in the sun. One surfaces with a thrashing fish, tips it up and swallows it headfirst.

I wish I were a cormorant. I'd gobble fish after fish. Fuego must miss being able to catch fish for himself. He depends on Magnus for everything, just as Pogo depends on me.

The sun tracks to the west and the day winds down. My eyes are burning and I'm thinking that I have to close them when I see a glint to the north—another vessel's windshield reflecting the sunshine.

But the hope that spurts into me crumbles fast. I don't even bother with the cover. The boat's too far away.

The sun begins to settle. I put my sweatshirt back on. I keep watch over an empty ocean.

I have been staring at the horizon when I realize that I am looking at a container ship making its way along the eastern horizon on a southerly course, its massive black hull and its white superstructure set aft, as big as a floating building in the late afternoon sun. Its deck is chockablock with rust-red and white and pale gray and green containers stacked nearly as high as the pilothouse windows.

It's out in the Great South Channel, the shipping lanes, too far away.

I watch it till it is a dot in the glare to the south, then nothing.

I try to take my mind off the grip of pain in my stomach, the grit of thirst in my mouth, by thinking about walking along the beach with Pogo before he had the lump, before he got old, and how he would run. He was a running machine. He bit at the foamy lips of the waves. He churned up sprays of sand as he tore around in circles. I would throw him a tennis ball and he would rocket straight down the beach after it, snag it, then spin and rocket back toward me along the wet flat of the beach, racing his reflection, his tongue lolling, his ears rippling, till I was sure he'd plow right into me, but he'd veer off at the last second and throw himself to a stop, his hindquarters raised and the ball between his forepaws. He'd whip his tail as if daring me to get the ball away from him.

Now even on a good day he has trouble walking. I wonder how much pain he's in, especially since he hasn't had his pills.

The shriek of gulls pulls me out of my daydream. Herring gulls and great black-backed gulls and gannets swarm above the water like a whirl of confetti, the gannets tucking their wings and diving like missiles and sending up spouts of white water, diving after baitfish driven toward the surface by some large fish.

The air brings me the scent of watermelon. Steve always said striped bass smelled like that. Striped bass. The second time. And I still can't catch one.

I picture a chunky white-fleshed filet, seared and steaming, the way Magnus made it. My mouth tries to water but can't. My stomach feels like a fist.

The birds follow the school off to the northwest, leaving only the shearwaters to swoop and bank through the low troughs and over the crests on their stiff albatross-like wings.

To the north I see a shape on the horizon.

I keep my eyes on it till it materializes into a tug towing a barge, the barge low in the water from its load of fuel oil and kicking up a white froth of a bow wake as it pushes through the water. The tug is about three barge-lengths ahead of it, leaving a trail of black fumes from its stack.

At this distance I cannot make out the tow cable.

I wonder if that's the same one—the one that almost sank us.

The shadow cast by the wreck lengthens across the water, and still I keep watch, my arms and legs trembling with the effort of holding on as I perch on the lip of the bow.

The sway of the wreck in the wave wash slows as the sea calms. From the southeast, plumes of thin white cloud begin to fan out across the sky. The sunlight softens, then goes dull. The water turns a glassy gray-green.

I try to lick my lips but my tongue catches on the scabby skin. My tongue feels barbed like a cat's. I look out over the water at the smudge that is Malabar and keep my eyes on it. No boat, no plane, nothing moves in that direction, nothing but the scalloped sea.

The sun turns brassy as it sinks toward the island. I watch it slip away and dissolve into a thin band of cloud.

I'm not going to make it. But what else can I do but wait—wait for the end like Pogo? Does he know that's what he's waiting for?

A wail from down below snaps me back.

"Okay, Pogo! It's okay. I'm coming."

Pogo is standing up, and when he spots me approaching his body gyrates, his tail windmilling. He's so excited he finds the spunk to do his pogo-stick bounce.

I crawl into the compartment beside him, patting his

head, and kneel down in front of him to knead his neck. "Do we have any more water?" I lean over to check the cup. The cup is empty. A spider has spun a small web across its mouth. The spider is gone, or hiding.

I sit down with my back to the wall, a shiver trickling over me. Sunburned. Now I'm sunburned, too. I rest my head against the steel and look up through the hatchway as Pogo comes up to me and presses his head against my knees.

The blue is gone, covered by a smoky grayness.

I don't know what to do.

Chapter Twenty-Three

A form appears in the hatchway.

A cormorant—the one-eyed one—is peering down at us. It holds something in its beak.

I sit up. What is it?

The bird tosses its head and flicks the object into the air. The thing cartwheels up, then falls down through the hatchway. With a wet slap, a six-inch mackerel lands on the floor beside us.

Pogo jumps back, his tail curled and stiff, his hackles raised. The fish rattles and flips, twisting and writhing, jittering on the floor as it tries to escape.

Fish. Fresh fish.

I shoot out my hand and pin the fish against the metal. Its tail beats on the deck. I grab the fish around the base of its tail, lift it up and smack its head down. It convulses, quivering. I smack it down again. The fish goes still.

For a moment I look at the fish I hold in my hand, its metallic blue and black bands and silvery undersides. It smells as fresh as the sea.

Pogo leans forward to touch his nose to its tail.

I look up. The cormorant is gone.

I fight an urge to bring the fish to my mouth and rip it apart with my teeth and chomp it down.

No. I'm not a cormorant. I'm not Pogo. Gut it first. Then cut it into chunks.

I pull my jackknife out of my pocket and clamp the fish by

the eye sockets with my thumb and forefinger. I kneel down and lay the fish on the floor. I flip it over to expose the belly, then thrust the tip of the knife into the skin below the gills.

It's a tinker mackerel. That's what Dad calls these small ones. Great eating and full of nutrients, he says. He grills them whole after he guts them. I love them, second only to striped bass.

I drive the knife in halfway and work it downward to slit the belly down to the vent. I reach inside and grab the cold guts and tug, tug again and tear the organs free. I hold the stomach in my palm. It's packed with sand eels. I poke the membrane with the tip of my knife. The mackerel just had dinner. Now it's our dinner. I slit the stomach sac so I can pluck out a pair of sand eels. I separate them and put one in my mouth, the other in my palm for Pogo.

I close my eyes and bite down, fish oil seeping into my mouth, the small sliver of silver fish mashed between my teeth, the taste of salt water and sardine-like flesh soothing my parched mouth.

I swallow.

Food. Food at last.

Pogo presses his snout to my hand and slurps up the fish.

I dig the rest of the eels out of the stomach and split them between us, gobbling them down like french fries. Then I lay the mackerel on its side.

Steve told me once, after he read a handbook about survival at sea, that a fish's eyes are a good source of fluid. I wish I had that book now. I know we need fluid, so I work the tip of the knife around a socket and gouge out the eyeball and pop it into my mouth.

For a moment I fight the gag rising in my throat. I take a breath.

Pretend it's a peppermint, I tell myself. I work the eyeball between my molars and chomp down. Gunk spurts into my mouth. I double over but chew fast and swallow. Glue and gristle. Chewy and slimy. No big deal.

I dig out the other eyeball and set it in my palm.

"Here you go, boy."

Pogo sucks it down.

I score a line along the fish's spine, slice downward to section the flesh, then slide the knife along the ribs. I cut one strip and put it in my mouth.

The deep red flesh tastes fresh and rich and sweet. Sashimi.

But I can't chew through the skin and scales. I gnaw on the piece to pull the flesh away from the skin.

"You're going to like this, Pogo." He's watching me as if I'm performing a magic trick. He hums and stutter-steps in place.

I cut the rest of the first side of the fish, splitting the chunks between us.

Flipping it over, I set to work on the other side. I feel each chunk go down my throat and land next to the others on the cave floor of my stomach. My stomach chirps in celebration. Pogo sniffs at the skeleton I hold in my hand, looking for more.

"That's it." I move to the opening and toss the guts and the rack into the dimness. I hear a splash and then another deeper splash and slap. Something was waiting down there.

For a moment the thought of what is waiting almost makes the fish in my stomach come back up.

I wipe my hands and knife on the cover, then tug Pogo to me as I sit back and wrap the cover around us. I cannot worry about something waiting in the water below. We're safe. For now. My stomach wants more. I hear it grinding as it works away at the fish. Food at last.

Thanks to the one-eyed cormorant.

I picture the bird tossing the fish into the compartment to us. That was just a mistake, I'm sure. It got scared and dropped its catch. Or did it? The bird almost seemed to be making a gift to us, as if it knew we were starving.

I stare into the dimming light around us. The water clucks and chuckles around the hull, the sea resting.

Then another sound, coming from outside the wreck. A buzzing.

The thin buzzing of an outboard motor.

Chapter Twenty-Four

I fly up the ladder so fast I do not feel the steps underfoot.

I stop. Standing in the open at the top of the hatchway, I can hear the rasp of the motor closing toward the wreck. I scan the water and spot the red and green running lights of a small boat approaching in the twilight.

I open my mouth to yell but only a croak comes out. I am almost blacking out from excitement and fear.

From below I hear Pogo's toenails scrabbling, and he lets out a wail.

I know I must make myself visible somehow, since even if I manage to call out, whoever is in the boat might not hear me over the sound of the motor.

"Stay, Pogo!" I yell down. "It's okay." Then I leap across the deck to grab on to the nearest stanchion. I have to get to the bow before the boat passes. Down here, I'm invisible against the dark shape of the wreck. I have to show myself against the sky.

Don't break, I think to myself as I claw my way from stanchion to stanchion. *Please hold*—the stanchions and my arm. I can see the boat is even closer. But it could pass right by just like *Miss Fortune*.

The cormorants fly away from me as I scramble higher, the buzzing of the motor louder now.

I reach the top and push myself as high as I can. I look down at the water below and dizziness sweeps over me. I blink and grip the rail and look down at the boat.

"Up here!" I scream.

I lock my feet between the rail and a stanchion and raise myself and wave my arms over my head.

The sound of the motor stays steady, the boat only fifty feet away.

Is it passing by?

"Hey!" I yell out. "Hey! Hey!"

Then I realize that the boat is swinging alongside.

"Up here! It's me! I'm here!"

The motor slows to an idle, and I can see a figure in the boat stand up.

My name comes to me over the water. "Sam? Is that you?"

That voice, I recognize that voice. That voice forces a sound out of my chest that is half laughter and half sob, a sound that echoes through the wreck. "Magnus!"

I am saved.

We are saved.

Magnus has saved us.

"I'm coming down!" I yell, even Pogo's cries unable to stop laughter from cackling out of me, making me sound like I've lost my mind, and maybe I have, I'm crazy with relief and happiness.

I find myself on the deck at the edge of the water. Magnus is standing in the rocking boat, five feet away. I can see his white hair and the outline of his hat and the flap of Fuego's wings on his shoulder. I want to fling myself right across the water into the boat.

"Sam, are you okay?"

"I'm okay. I'm okay."

"You're going home," says Magnus. "We'll get you home."

"Pogo. I need to get Pogo."

As the boat begins to drift away, Magnus steps to the bow. He's holding a coil of line.

"Let me throw this to you," he says.

I wave as I move toward the water.

"Ready?" he calls.

I brace myself against the deck. "Ready."

He tosses the line and it loops into the air and flops over my shoulder. "Got it."

Tie it right, I say to myself as I hitch it to a stanchion. *Take a breath and check it.* I cinch it tight and look back at Magnus. He moves aft and cuts the motor. The quiet returns along with the sound of a swell gurgling in the hull. A gull screams.

"Where's Pogo?" he says. "Is he okay?"

I nod. "Below," I say. "I'll get him."

"Do you need help?"

I think for a moment. If two of us haul him up from the compartment, we could get aboard Magnus's boat faster. Bringing him down the deck alone, a rust-covered and guano-slimed forty-five-degree slope a good fifteen feet above the water, I could lose my grip on his harness—or my footing.

"Might make sense," I say. "The deck's kind of steep."

He smiles. "Coming over."

He reaches for the line and pulls his small boat alongside. The boat lists under his weight as he moves to the bow. He steps up on a seat and puts one foot on the rail, and the boat dips low.

"Here I come," he says.

He sucks in a deep breath and bends his knees, holding his hands out to his sides for balance. Fuego rises and flutters. Magnus stays in that position for a moment as he judges his jump. I think how being so big isn't always an advantage just as he lets out a stream of breath and rocks backward. At the same moment I spot a swell rolling in from the gloom, but before I can call out, Magnus leaps.

The swell trips the boat, shoving Magnus high into the air, and sends him hurtling onto the steel plates of the wreck. The sound he makes as he hits freezes me—a short gull-like squawk. He slides downward, lunging for one of the stanchions. I hear the stanchion snap. He groans as he starts to slide sideways, pawing for a grip, and comes to a stop just above the water. Fuego flaps up and lands on the deck above him.

Magnus's boat whirls away, then swerves back, stopped by the line.

"Magnus!"

I can see him grimacing, his chest heaving. He's so close to the edge that his right arm splashes into the water.

"Magnus?"

He pulls his arm out of the water. "A minute," he gasps. "Give me a minute."

A swell could sweep in and wash him off. I need to do something. Fast.

He tips his head back, grimacing. His hat is missing— must have fallen overboard but I can't make it out on the water. Fuego flutters and tries to land on Magnus's chest, then lands back on the deck.

"Get Pogo," says Magnus through clenched teeth. "We need to . . ." He pauses, then exhales. "We need to get on the boat while we still have a chance."

He lets out a stream of air.

I wonder how I can I get him back onto the boat, this giant of a man. I look at the silhouette of the boat riding off the wreck, and I know that to try to get him into it is to risk falling into the water.

I reach the lip of the hatchway. Before I climb down, I look back at Magnus sprawled below at the edge of the water.

"Do you think you can stand?" I call down to him. "Is it your leg?"

He points down at his ankle. Even that effort makes him squeeze his eyes shut and bang his head back on the deck.

"The same one," I say, "from before?"

He makes a small motion of his head that I take to be a nod.

I wonder if he is in shock. When I broke my arm, the pain

made me feel as if I were floating. My world was the pain, and nothing else seemed to exist.

Darkness surrounds us now. Not a single star shows overhead.

I'm rooted to the lip of the hatchway. I know I should go below to get Pogo, but Magnus is lying at the edge of the water. I shouldn't leave him alone even though he told me to get Pogo.

But I have to. Otherwise we'll be stuck.

I swing my leg over into the hatchway. I go down two steps of the ladder. Pogo hums from below. I stop to peer over the lip of the hatchway to check on Magnus one last time.

I see him sitting up and for a second I think that's a good sign, but then I realize that he's trying to get above a swell rising around him. He raises his arms as the water keeps coming.

I vault back up out of the hatchway and scuttle down, scraping through the flakes of rust and patches of guano to reach him just as the water is rising around his waist and lifting him away. I see his face, his mouth open, and I find a stanchion and latch on to it with one hand and to the front of his shirt with the other. His weight pulls me down toward the water and I feel my fingers cramping with the effort to hold on to his shirt. My arms are stretching wider as the water pulls him out. Which will give out first—the bone in the arm I'm holding him with or the stanchion I'm clinging to with the other?

Then I hear the water gurgling as the swell recedes. I feel Magnus's weight settle. At last he comes to rest on the deck, water streaming around him into the sea as he slumps back.

My chest is heaving. I know we need to get higher up on the deck, maybe even climb below to give him a chance to recover.

"Can . . . you . . . stand?" I pant.

He groans and slides his left foot under him and pushes himself up on the deck.

"We have to get above the waterline," I say. "Can you do that again? I'll pull you up."

Fuego flaps his wings, tries to land on Magnus, then hops to the deck and chitters.

"It's okay, Fuego," I say.

Magnus moves his mouth but no sound comes out. I know I have to get him to safety. Getting onto his boat will have to wait. He keeps his right leg extended as he pushes with his other foot. This time he stiffens his arm and I pull it up at the same time he pushes off, and he slides up.

I can hear his breath coming in gravelly gasps. One, two, three more pushes and we're still only halfway.

I don't want to look at his ankle. I imagine it twisted or bent and swelling fast. Or maybe the bone has ripped right through the skin.

I hear Pogo wail.

"Ready?" I ask Magnus.

He pushes off with his foot again and we creep higher, Fuego hopping and flapping after us, creeping higher as the darkness seems to deepen until at last we reach the lip.

As we rest, I can feel gravity trying to pull him back down the deck and I keep a firm hold on his arm. Now I must figure out how to get him down the incline of the steps.

"Can you swing your legs around?" I say. "Can you sit up?"

He grunts, then tries to raise himself. I place my hand on his broad back and push.

He sits up, puffing, then drops his head, his hand gripping my arm as if to squeeze it till it pops off.

"The ladder, Magnus. It's right here. We have to get down below."

I take hold of his good leg and help him swing it around so he can feel for the ladder. Then I scramble around onto the ladder in front of him.

"Slide down slow from step to step," I say. "Lean forward and put your weight on me. Don't worry."

I hear Pogo below us humming.

Magnus rests his hands on my shoulders and I feel his weight pressing me down.

His weight is growing and so is my momentum and I grab for a handhold and then my shoes slip and my feet go out from underneath me and I skid down the rest of the steps onto the floor.

Somehow he has gripped on to the ladder and eases himself down.

My thigh throbs as I pick myself up and grab his arm to guide him to the floor and help him lie on his back.

"Are you okay?" I say to him.

I hear him exhale and then I hear a whir come down the steps, and Fuego appears beside him. All I can make out is a pale form moving around by Magnus's head.

Pogo is sniffing Magnus and he's wagging his tail so hard it flogs me.

"Easy, boy. He's hurt."

I lay the cover over Magnus, then reach down and loosen the laces on his right boot.

"I'm not sure what I can do. It's too dark to see your ankle. Maybe you should elevate it or something."

I hear his ragged breathing.

I reach out for Pogo, pull him to me and dig my fingers into his fur.

"Just try to rest, Magnus. Tomorrow we'll . . ." I start to say that tomorrow we'll find a way to get on his boat and make our way to help.

But I don't know if that's possible.

Chapter Twenty-Five

The first drops land on my face with such a light touch that all I do is brush at them with my hand and turn over on my side and reach out to feel Pogo sleeping beside me. I shift again and bang my knee against the wall. I open my eyes and turn to look up at the hatchway.

A raindrop plops on my forehead, and then another follows. I pull Pogo closer.

Raindrops click on the vinyl cover.

Then I remember: Magnus is under the cover. I hear him breathing beside me in the compartment. I'm glad I have the cover for him. It's like a tent and will keep him dry, or at least mostly dry. But it's not big enough for all of us.

I sit up and slide farther beneath the overhang and pull Pogo with me.

The soft clicking of the raindrops on the cover begins to lull me. I hug Pogo closer for his warmth. The raindrops hitting on the floor splash onto my pants, but mostly I'm dry. I feel my eyes turn to lead and slide closed.

The rain means we'll have a good, long drink of water.

At that moment the rain changes to a downpour. I hear the rain drumming down on the cover.

"Magnus?" I say. He doesn't respond.

"Magnus!"

He grunts.

"Are you okay? It's raining."

"I know."

"Can you move over here? It's out of the rain."

I kneel and pull him as he hunches into the small rectangle of shelter beneath the overhang.

"Better?" I say.

"Yes," he says, his voice a near whisper.

"Can I do anything for you?"

"Nothing," he says. "Nothing to be done. In the morning . . ."

I gather the cover around him and draw my knees up to try to stay out of the rain.

I hear drips landing in the flashlight cap. On deck, water begins gurgling as the rain comes on harder.

I begin to hear water everywhere: drips and drops in the compartment, scratching and gurgling above, trickling and tinkling and rattling all around us.

"I'm sorry," he whispers. "This is not—"

"Magnus," I say. "Don't be. I mean, I'm the one . . . I'll figure it out. We'll get in your boat in the morning and get you back."

"I knew . . . I knew you might try to take Pogo away. And then the Coast Guard plane . . . it had to be looking for your boat. They would never have guessed you were here. Fuego and I came out looking, just a hunch. But where is your boat? What happened to it?"

I look away. How can I tell him?

"I let . . . I let it go," I whisper, looking back at him. "By mistake. The knot I tied didn't stay . . . it didn't stay tied."

He makes a short groan.

"Magnus?"

"Worse," he says, his voice strained. "This is worse than the first time. The pain. I need to . . . can't talk right now."

"Okay. Just rest. I wish I could . . ."

I wish I could help him. But I can't. All we can do is wait.

The sound of rain fills my ears as it churns down in waves, one moment a waterfall roar, then tapering to a whisper, then pouring down again. Drips form a sheet from the lip of the hatchway. The rain releases the scent of rust and guano and salt and seawater and seaweed so that the compartment takes on a musk like an aquarium.

I feel along the floor for the cup, reaching beyond the protection of the overhang.

In moments my arm is soaked.

I nudge the cup with my fingertips and grab it.

"Magnus," I say. "Water. Hold out your hand."

I find his hand and slip the cup in it, and I hear a slurp. Then he hands the cup back and I hold it out again and in moments it fills up. I bring it to my lips. I swallow half of it, then hold the cup out for Pogo. Rainwater splashes down around us. He laps it up.

I see the lighter form of Fuego on the floor, sipping water from a puddle.

Collect more. Somehow. What will I put it in? Can I collect it anywhere else on the ship?

I think about using the cover as a funnel for the rain, but I have no idea what to funnel it into. And I don't want Magnus to get soaked.

I could fill the flashlight itself.

As I feel around for it, I hear a wave wash into the hull. The wreck sways. Air puffs down from above and splashes raindrops across my face.

I locate the flashlight and take out the dead batteries and set them on the floor.

I lean out and hold the empty flashlight up to the rainwater cascading down. Without the protection of the overhang, I'm so soaked that water drips from my elbows.

I begin to shiver. The rain comes on harder, and another wave sweeps around the wreck.

I can feel the flashlight filling, and then I duck back beneath the overhang.

"More?" I say to Magnus.

"No."

I take a drink, then tip the flashlight for Pogo. He laps the water till the flashlight is dry.

A wave approaches with the sound of a hurtling railroad car and crashes around us. The wreck groans. Another wave breaks against the hull. The wreck screeches from deep within.

The rain hammers on the deck above us, and gusts of wind shriek and moan in the fissures of the hull. The sound of breaking waves becomes a continuous roaring in my ears. I feel Pogo quivering beside me. Magnus is quiet except for a groan now and then.

I wish he would not just lie there. I wish he would stand up and tell us how to save ourselves.

Another wave breaks against the wreck, and the hull trembles and squeals. I press harder against the wall, away from the rainwater streaming down.

In the darkness the forces around us seem to take on monstrous proportions. I picture green waves rising up to the height of the bow before dropping their tons of seawater against the creaking wreck. Could the wreck break apart? Could the waves push it off the shoal till it was swallowed up?

I feel the wreck swaying, its motion constant. With the breaking waves and pounding rain surrounding us, I have the sensation that the wreck is making headway through the water, on a course unknown.

A wave slams against the hull, and the wreck bucks and groans. I grab onto Pogo to steady myself. Saltwater spray mixed with torrents of rain falls down on us.

If we were in *Scallop*, a wave probably would have sunk us by now. Poor boat. I wonder if she's still floating. Will I ever see her again?

At least *Scallop* stands a chance. She'll keep riding into the wind—if she doesn't get swamped and sink.

Another wave sends a quiver through the wreck.

An image of the cormorant clutching onto the end of the

broken mast comes to me. Is the bird still there? What does it do in a storm? Will it survive? The more I think about the bird, the more I want to be sure it is okay. I want to thank the bird.

I look up at the darkness above, the spray and rainwater icy against my face. I hear the wind whine and moan. I wish I could climb up and crawl out on the mast and gather up the bird in my arms and bring it down into the compartment where it would be safe, or at least safer. I could offer it some shelter, some kindness, the way the Magnus did to us.

The way the bird offered us help.

But I cannot help the bird.

My shoes and clothes are sopping and waves of shivers sweep over me. Dry socks. That's all I want. Dry, warm socks and dry pants and a ski parka and ski hat and mittens. My red and black plaid wool jacket. A mug of hot cocoa to wrap my hands around. My oilskin jacket and pants. A woodstove with a blazing fire.

I hear the wave. I brace myself.

Magnus groans.

"Hang on," I whisper. A mountain of stones is pouring toward us. The grinding roar overwhelms the sounds of the other waves, the rain, the wind. It fills my ears with a crushing crackling as the pressure thickens in the compartment. I feel the wreck stagger and cold seawater gush down on top of us. More and more of it rises around me as I stand up, water swirling up to my ankles, my calves.

The water keeps coming.

"Come here," I say to Pogo. I swing around to the ladder and pull myself up above the level of the water, then reach back and haul him up after me, his legs paddling in the air till his paws find a step. I hear water pouring out through the open doorway into the water below. Rain batters my head.

Then I jump down and grab Magnus and haul him upright, his weight crushing down on me.

He shouts in pain as I push him onto the ladder.

"Water's coming in!" I shout. "We have to climb up. A few steps."

He uses the knee of his bad leg to hike himself up and his good leg to steady himself on each step. I follow him, pushing against his back to help him climb. He struggles up two, three steps to where Pogo is. Fuego flaps to his shoulder.

Another wave slams the wreck, shooting water from below through the doorway and from over the top through the hatchway, sending waterfalls of seawater over us.

"Hold on tight," I say to Magnus.

I feel the wreck shift, the angle of the ladder now steeper. I clutch onto Pogo's harness. I steel myself for the next wave to charge into the wreck, fear weakening my grip. I know that another rush of water could wash us off the ladder, out of the compartment and through the doorway into the water below.

Where something is waiting for us.

If we get washed overboard and don't drown in the waves, a mouth filled with teeth is sure to find us.

Raindrops and salt spray rake across us with the sound of flying nails. We huddle against the ladder. I lean my hip against one of the steps until it goes numb. Then I shift to the other side, keeping a tight grip on Pogo.

No way that bird is alive.

I cling to the ladder, listening to the waves roar and crash. I wait for the next wave to thunder down on us and wrench the wreck into the ocean.

Below us, I hear water running with the sound of an over-flowing brook. I sense that the water filling the compartment is draining out.

I decide to test it. I unhook my arm from around the ladder rail. It's stiff from being locked in one position, and I have to flex it before I let myself down to the floor.

"Pogo," I call. "You stay."

I splash into water only up to my ankles, and the level is

dropping fast. I climb back up for Pogo, then help Magnus back down and settle him beneath the overhang. The waves crash and boom against the hull as the wind seethes around it. The wreck quivers and pitches.

I squeeze my eyes closed and feel each second pass, convinced that soon another wave will hurl itself down to swamp us and carry the wreck away. Pressing against the wall, I fold my arms around Pogo, waiting, listening to the waves, the wind, the wreck.

Then, from above, I hear metal crack and then a boom vibrates through the wreck.

My heart lurches.

The bird. The bird's roost. Something must have happened.

Chapter Twenty-Six

I have to see.

"Stay here," I tell Pogo. "Magnus, I have to go topside." I don't have time to explain. "I just . . . I'll be back."

I claw my way up the ladder. Rain rakes me as I near the top. My shoulder hits something hard in the darkness above the hatchway. I reach out and feel a solid round pole lying on the diagonal across the hatchway. I peer into the blackness. It's the mast. The wind has blown it down. The cormorant was at the end of it—had been.

A gust shoves me as I squeeze past the mast. I crouch, clenching the lip of the hatchway. The waves hiss and rush and roar as they pour past or break against the hull, louder than when I was down below.

Where is the bird? Where could it have gone?

From below I hear a sound. I set my feet on the mast. It shifts, then holds. The sound comes again—a weak grunting. Is that it? Is that it down there?

I feel my way down the deck, the mast giving as I lean my weight against it. Rainwater streams past. A gust bashes against me, slashing rain across my face. I stop to listen.

There—just below me. The sound comes again, a single feeble grunt beneath the roar of the wind and waves.

I let myself down farther, hearing the breaking of the waves reach higher.

Again I hear it. Below me, I make out a darker shape

against the hull above the breakers. I reach down and feel wet feathers under my fingers. *There you are.*

I cup my hand around the bird and pull it toward me. I feel its body stiffen, a wing extend and then go limp.

With one hand I scoop the bird against my body. It's tense and rigid but not fighting me. It drapes its long neck and head over my shoulder, its tail reaching below my waist.

"Hold on," I say in a low voice. I feel the raging beat of the bird's heart against my chest as I climb. I clutch the bird to me with one hand and use the other to pull myself toward the hatchway.

Don't slip. Take it easy. I push my way along the length of the mast till I reach the hatchway, then swing my legs over the lip. I take the first steps down and squeeze past the mast.

The bird twists. I tighten my hold. "Almost there."

The bird calms as we descend, the outside sounds quieter down in the compartment.

My feet hit the floor and Pogo rushes up to press his nose against me, then the tail of the bird.

"It's okay, Pogo. It's our friend."

"Are you all right?" says Magnus. "What did you do?"

I pull the bird closer to me as I sit down against the wall.

"I had to save it," I whisper, my heart rattling in my chest. "A cormorant. It helped us. It gave us . . . it gave us food."

The bird arches its neck and struggles to spread its wings. It's warm against my drenched shirt, its chest trilling with its speeding heart. It lets out a weak grunt.

"*Phalacrocorax auritus*," whispers Magnus. "Double-crested cormorant."

I sit down beneath the overhang and hold the bird to me, rain spattering against the cover.

Pogo leans against me.

"Good boy," I whisper. "It's okay."

The bird shivers. It lets out a small groan.

"Don't be scared." My voice is almost drowned out by the rain and wind and the creaking of the wreck.

Another crash of a wave and a tearing of metal make me reach out and pull Pogo closer to me, and hold the bird tight.

"Magnus," I say. "Are you all right?"

He clears his throat.

"A hospital ship," he whispers. "You are running a hospital ship, Sam."

I wish, I want to say to him, I wish I really were running a hospital ship, and that I could make everything all right.

The longer we wait, the quieter the world around us becomes. The wreck's swaying begins to slow. The wind goes from a shriek to a mumble to a sigh. The rain patters, trickles, ceases, leaving only thousands of drips. The waves crackle, wash, splash. Magnus groans in his sleep, but at least he sleeps.

The bird stops shivering.

"That's better," I whisper.

Is it sleeping? Is it alive?

Once, I found a fledgling starling in the backyard by the hydrangea bush. It squatted helpless in the grass, working its beak, its scruffy feathers like a tiny dust mop. I ran inside and dug a shoebox out of my closet. I took the shoebox back out and gathered the bird in my hands and put it inside. I plucked grass and a few leaves and made a shelter for it inside the box. For a day I fed it worms and grubs and gave it water from an eyedropper. Steve looked in at the bird and shook his head. "It's a goner," he said. That evening I set the shoebox beside my bed. I peered in at the bird. It was a ball of fluff backed into a corner among the leaves and grass, its heartbeat ruffling its feathers. It blinked at me and held its beak open for food.

I put the lid on the box. I had poked air holes in it with my jackknife. I climbed into bed and switched off the lamp. I listened for any sound coming from the shoebox as I stayed as still as I could beneath the covers. I woke up several times during the night, listening.

In the morning I rolled over and reached down and removed the lid. The bird was lying on its side, its eyes open and blank like a doll's, its spindly legs stiff. When I touched it, it was cold.

"You'll live," I whisper to the cormorant. "Won't you?"

I feel its heartbeat.

Sometime hours into the night, I look up through the hatchway and see a star. One star. I stand up in slow motion and take hold of one of the ladder rails and pull myself up, the bird pressed to me. Emerging from the hatchway, I feel the breeze around me, a sweet, watery flow coming from a new direction.

Where's the mast? The broken mast is gone. All that remains is a ragged hole that has been torn out of the deck. That's what made the big noise. The bird would have died.

More stars appear between the breaking clouds. They look bright-eyed and polished. The clouds glide past and turn white as the moon appears.

I listen to the waves. By the moonlight I can see their dark shapes rolling by. Now and then the wreck rocks.

Another night. We made it through another night. And Magnus is with us. Alive. And so is the bird.

But will it stay alive? I have nothing to feed it. I have nothing to feed Pogo. I have nothing to feed Fuego. Or Magnus.

The bird makes a small groan. "Let's go back down," I say, kneeling before the hatchway. "We'll rest."

Can I save it?

Can I save all of us?

Chapter Twenty-Seven

I wake to see a rectangle of gray dawn light through the hatchway.

Steve told me that when the sun is still fifteen degrees below the horizon and objects are taking on shape but the horizon is still indistinct, that's called "nautical twilight."

I wonder what time nautical twilight is. All I can see is the grainy gray light seeping into the compartment. Is it five? Five thirty? Maybe later?

Hunger stabs me like an ice pick and drives the thought from my mind. My hand strays over Pogo's soft head lying on my lap. I begin thinking about him, about what will happen when he's gone. Will he become something else, maybe a cormorant? What will happen to Fuego? And Magnus—will he become a bird? And what has Steve become? I don't know. I only know that I have to save Pogo somehow.

Then I realize that I am no longer holding the bird.

I throw off the cover and see in the dimness that my pants are splotched with guano.

The body of the bird stretches in a low, dark lump in the corner. Fuego is standing beside the cormorant, watching over it. I crawl over to it and lay my hand on the bird's breast. Fuego hops away to stand beside Magnus. I hear Magnus gag with a jagged snore. The bird does not move. I press down against the feathers. A heartbeat trembles against my hand.

"Don't die," I whisper.

I look around me, my own heart thudding. Pogo struggles to his feet and limps over to me. I take his head in my hands.

I have no food for us.

I don't know what's wrong with the bird.

Wait. Water. Maybe it needs water.

I rest my hand on the bird and look around the compartment. The flashlight cap must have been washed away.

"Wait here," I say. "Hang on."

I crawl across the floor, patting the wet metal deck ahead of me to feel for the cap. No way it's here. I follow the wall till I reach the spot where I set it. Not there. I crawl farther, feeling toward the corner. What's that?

My fingers bump an object. I open them, then let them close around it. The cap. Filled with water.

I bring it back to the bird and sit down. I cradle the bird's head in my lap. "Try this," I say. "A little sip."

I lift the bird's beak with one hand and spread it apart with my fingers. The bird does not resist. I dribble a few drops on its tongue.

"More?" I let a few more drops roll down the bird's throat. The bird shakes and shifts its wings. It opens its beak. I see that the edges are serrated with rows of small teeth.

"All of it?"

I swirl the remaining water around in the cup, then bring it to the bird's beak and let the rest of the water trickle into its throat. I should have let the flashlight fill with water, too.

The bird clacks its beak and raises its head, craning its neck away from me as if to look at me with its one good eye.

"Better?" I say, a warmth flowing from some hidden source within me.

The feeling subsides when I look at Pogo.

"Sorry, pal," I say. "We'll have to wait for our turn."

The bird bends its head to pluck at its breast feathers.

Magnus lifts his head and pushes himself up on one elbow.

"How is . . ." he says, wiping a hand over his face. "How is the bird?"

"Okay," I say. "What about you?"

"Not . . . so . . . good."

I crawl to him to check his ankle. "Okay if I look?" I ease back the cuff of his pant leg, then roll down the sand-colored sock stretched around the ankle. Beneath it, the ankle looks like a white sausage mottled with dark stains. But I see no blood.

"The bone didn't break the skin," I say. "At least I don't think so."

He nods again. "Can't move it."

"Don't worry," I say. "We'll get you off the wreck. It's getting light."

He pulls himself to a sitting position.

"The bird," he says, "is better off topside. It needs to fly, to fish. It needs the air, as I do, but I cannot move. Not now."

Fuego chitters and flaps his wings.

"See if it can fly," he says. "I would have done the same . . . the same for Fuego."

"Yes," I say. "To free it."

Magnus nods. "If the waves have subsided enough, go aboard my boat. Get the radio in the locker below the stern seat." Then he rests his head back against the wall.

A radio. We can call for help. I picture a Coast Guard helicopter hovering over us, lowering a basket for Magnus, for me. For Pogo.

First I must help the bird. I reach out to it, whispering, "It's okay."

The bird opens its wings, then folds them.

"I'm not going to hurt you." I rest my hands on the bird's wings. I feel them try to lift.

"It's okay. I'm just going to carry you topside."

I gather the bird to me. It tries to wrench out of my grasp.

"Hang on. I'll let you go in a sec."

When we reach the top, I hear Pogo hum from below. "I'll be right back for you, boy."

Fresh air sweeps over me. I look around and make out the form of the wreck, now dismasted, its bow appearing to lean at a sharper angle toward starboard. So the hull did shift during the storm. No telling how long it'll stay above the water.

The stars fade. To the east, pale blue shows along the horizon.

The bird makes a grunting sound and tries to flex its wings. I set it on the slanted deck. It opens its wings and nuzzles its breast feathers.

"Better up here, isn't it?" I say.

A flutter of wings makes me turn around. A dark form flaps past the wreck, circles, then swoops up to land on the port rail.

"Your friends are there," I say to the bird.

The bird watches another cormorant fly past. Will it take off? Is it okay?

The breeze breathes from the northeast, riffling the water.

In a flurry of wings, the bird launches itself off the deck and swoops down toward the water.

My heart catches.

The bird drops toward the surface.

"Fly!" I shout.

The bird flaps harder.

I close one eye.

Just as it nears the top of a swell, the bird gains altitude, flapping fast, begins to rise, and circles away into the grainy light.

I watch the sky where the bird had been.

Will it come back? Will I ever see it again?

The boat. Wasn't the boat on the port side of the wreck, the opposite side from where I had tied *Scallop*?

I work my way over to the rail. I can see the knot still secured to the stanchion. But when I look over the side, I do not know what I'm seeing. The line descends straight down the side of the hull. It's taut as a rod.

The boat is there, below the surface, at the end of the line. But not the entire boat. Only the bow remains, just underwater, bumping against the hull as the swells wash in.

The storm tore down the mast on the wreck, nearly killed the cormorant, almost wrenched the wreck from its resting place. Now it has destroyed Magnus's boat. I can see the line looped around the bow cleat, all that's holding the ripped planks and broken ribs of the bow section.

I stare down into the water, the shadowy shape of the wreckage filling me with pity for the boat. I picture her—the boat Magnus built—alone in the darkness, the wind and the waves hammering her to pieces against the black wall of the hull, the radio sinking into the depths. I hear gulls call in the distance, birds who are starting their day, a day like any other day for them.

I climb down into the compartment. Magnus opens his eyes and turns his head toward me. He has rolled up the cover and his ankle rests on it. I cannot bring myself to speak. All I can do is shake my head. I see him raise his eyebrows.

"The boat?" he whispers.

"The storm," I say, and wave my hand. "The storm sank your boat. Only the bow . . . only a piece of the bow is left." I shake my head again and go to Pogo. I kneel down in front of him and bury my face in the thick fur of his neck. "I need," I manage to say as I lift my head, "to go keep watch."

Fuego raises himself up on Magnus's shoulder and flaps his wings.

"Come on, boy. Let's go up." I take hold of Pogo's harness and hoist him up the ladder with me.

We climb through the hatchway and sit down, my heels set at the base of a stanchion to brace myself, my hand keeping a hold on Pogo's harness. I lean back to watch the last planet fade in the brightening blue. Which planet is it? Steve would know its name.

I hear more flapping and twist around to see a cormorant land on the bow rail above us. It spreads its wings. Now the light is bright enough for me to see that it isn't the one-eyed one.

I can see the horizon and three spear-shaped clouds turn purple, then pale pink.

Is anyone searching for us? I know the Coast Guard had been.

Full daylight overspreads the ocean. I feel the wreck sway in the small swells.

Another cormorant returns to land and spread its wings to dry. Then I see a crown of molten gold push above the eastern horizon and the sun flares up from behind the ocean. I squint in the glare as the sun shoots its rays over the rippled waves. Two more cormorants return, their feathers glistening with iridescence in the sunlight. The slow swells make the wreck creak and sway.

I sit upright, lean over the rail and look down at the green water rising along the hull to see if I can find the source of the creaking. When the swell recedes, I look along the waterline fouled with algae and bristling with barnacles. Barnacles. Why didn't I think of barnacles before? I could have fed the cormorant. I can feed Pogo. And myself. Can Magnus even stomach any food?

I remember that when Steve went to Spain in his senior year in high school, he said he had eaten a plate of big plump barnacles, a different kind from the ones around Fog Island. It was in Santiago de Compostela, the town at the end of the Way of St. James. The Way was a Roman trade route taken by pilgrims since the Middle Ages, and when the pilgrims looked up at the night sky, they followed the Milky Way since it ran in the same direction. Steve said that signs with a scallop-shell symbol marked the route.

Maybe I can reach some barnacles on the hull.

"Stay here, Pogo. Don't follow me."

I let myself down the incline of the rusted deck to just above the waterline. The swells are low but now and then a higher one sweeps in.

I pull my knife out of my pocket and flip open the blade. Rust is already forming in the steel housing. Gripping the last stanchion above the water with one hand, I bend down to reach the knife to where I see barnacles clustered on the hull. Even if I can scrape some off, I can't grab them this way.

I turn around and stretch myself out on the slanted deck, facing the water headfirst. I crook one leg around the stanchion and lower myself toward the water and the band of barnacles. A swell recedes and I reach out and scrape, the blade grating against the hull and dislodging a few barnacles no bigger than broken teeth. My hands splash in the water as a swell rises up the side. I pull myself back up to lean against the stanchion, cupping the barnacles in one hand. The shells are hard as porcelain, the edges toothed and razor-sharp.

I set the biggest one on the deck and lay the flat of the blade against it. Then I press the heel of my hand on the blade and crush the shell. I flick the shards of the shell into the water and pluck up the morsel of mashed meat that is more like pulverized mucus. I put it on my tongue, then bite down on it. I think of the barnacles Steve scraped off *Scallop*—how I'd never have dreamed of putting one in my mouth. This one releases a salty clam nuttiness. I swallow and spit out a crumb of shell.

It's okay, but I only need a thousand more to make a meal.

I turn around again and hook my leg around the stanchion. I let myself down toward the water and the green swell rises and keeps coming and I try to pull myself back up but the water keeps rising and then it bulges over my head and submerges me.

I open my eyes to see a shadow rising toward me, a shadow as big as my boat.

I push off the hull and claw out of the water and come up spitting and gasping to see a triangular dorsal fin cutting away just beyond the rail. Shaking, I climb back up the deck and take Pogo by the harness and sit on the rim of the hatchway. I gather him to me and sit staring at the slow swells rising and falling like a breathing body.

I keep my eyes pinned on the water where the shadow was.

Pogo curls up beside me, but still I keep my hand on his harness. The cormorants return and gulls fly high overhead and shearwaters veer over the smooth swells and gannets cruise in the distance. The sun climbs but I do not move. I am frozen in the sun. I do not dare move.

Then I hear a distant foghorn, and I start to stand up to look around, until I realize that it is Pogo snoring, the sound a soft hoot right at my feet.

The swells rise and fall. The sun reaches its peak and begins to slide to the west, and still I stare, mesmerized by the motion of the swells, the knowledge that we aren't going home.

I peer into the compartment to check on Magnus. I call his name. No response.

"Stay," I tell Pogo.

When I kneel beside Magnus, he slides his eyes open and looks up as if he doesn't know who I am.

"Are you okay?"

He closes his eyes and nods.

"I'm okay," he says at last, his voice cracking. "You?"

I nod.

"I should go back up."

"One minute," he says. "I need you to know something."

I lean against the metal wall. I wish I could lie down. I did not realize how tired I am from straining my eyes and holding on all day. For days.

"Your dog, Sam," he says, his voice almost a whisper. "You have looked after him well. You must know this. You have done what's right."

I turn my eyes to him. I feel ropes inside me loosening.

"My brother," I say. "My brother wanted me to. His last words to me . . . were that he wanted me to take care of him. That Pogo was my dog. His last words . . ."

He clears his throat. I see him grimace.

Then he exhales.

"Your brother," he says. "That he is gone is not your fault."

The day we cleaned *Scallop* on the beach comes back to me. Sitting on the boat's rail, I asked Steve why he had to go. Pogo lifted his head, blinking. Steve held the scraper loose in his hand as if he was weighing it. He looked out across the water, then back at me. "I don't expect you to understand," he said. "I have to see. For myself. That's all. I have to go . . . see over the wall. I have to know what's it's like. Combat"—he waved the scraper—"is only part of it." He squinted at me, then kneeled down again. Pogo rested his head back on the towel. "You just take care of Pogo," he said, the scraper grating against the hull. "I'll take care of myself."

I clear my throat.

I could not have stopped Steve from going. I cannot stop him from not coming back. But I believed I could have.

Magnus coughs. "Sam, listen to me." He draws his wrist across his mouth. "You will bring Pogo home. This you must believe."

At that moment Pogo lets out a cry.

"Magnus," I say, "I have to go."

I look at him.

"I just want to say . . ."

He holds my gaze.

Pogo cries again.

Magnus nods, then closes his eyes.

I head for the ladder.

I sit with Pogo, watching the water and the sky. The sun tracks lower.

In the distance to the east I see a geyser of spray, and then another beside it—two whales, free to make their way wherever they choose.

All the cormorants are back—all save one.

I take a deep breath and stand up. Pogo watches me. I can't take him up to the bow. But I have to go look.

"Just stay here," I tell him. "I'll be right back. Okay?"

He hums as I make my way up to the top of the wreck, the birds huddling away from me as I approach. They leap one by one off the rail and flap away.

I grip onto the topmost stanchion and look down to check on Pogo. I can hear him hum again, but at least he hasn't moved.

To the west I see the dash of Malabar on the horizon. To the north lies open water. To the south, the same. To the east, the same again.

The water is turning a deeper blue-green with flecks of gold as the sun dips toward Malabar. Another day gone. Another night ahead.

I look back to the east.

Is that another whale out there, spouting a white plume? Is it a whitecap? Why would only one whitecap appear? Why would a whale's spout stay in one place?

I blink. I look again at the jot of white. I close my eyes so they will not burn. When I open my eyes again, I see that the white object has moved closer.

My heart begins to dance.

A sailboat is heading our way.

Chapter Twenty-Eight

The shadow of the wreck stretches across the water, pointing toward the sail.

My own shadow lengthens down the slanted deck. I close my eyes again, fearing that when I open them the sail will not be there.

I open them.

The boat is there.

My boat. My boat is there, still afloat, moving closer.

My boat is back. *Scallop.* She has found her way back to me.

I watch, willing the boat closer.

She remains only a small white tooth in the middle distance between the wreck and the horizon. I've got to get out there. She could start drifting away again.

My stomach swoops, nausea for a moment replacing hunger.

I have no choice. I have to swim. I have to swim out to the boat.

I glance down at the heave of a swell rising up around the wreck. Pogo is now standing, looking up the deck at me, swaying.

"Hang tight, boy," I call. "I'll be right down. Don't move."

I hustle down, trying to be careful but wanting to get to Pogo fast. When I reach him he presses his head into my hands. I scratch him behind the ears, looking past him into the water. I see nothing below the surface except for the hull angling away.

I have to go. I have to swim for it. I have to tell Magnus.

But.

I look back down into the water. The shark will come for me.

If we stay on the wreck, how long will we last? How long before the wreck breaks apart and sinks? How long before we die of thirst? How long can Magnus hang on?

The boat is about three-quarters of a mile away, maybe half a mile. I don't know if I have the strength to swim that far.

I run my tongue over the sandpapery plates and crusted cracks of my lips. I look at a cormorant landing on the rim of the hatchway. It isn't the one-eyed one. I tell Pogo to wait and I let myself down to the bottom lip of the hatchway. The cormorant edges away to the port rail.

"Magnus," I say. A square of light frames his legs, the broken ankle resting on the rolled-up cover. "A boat's out there. My boat. I have to go . . . I have to go get it. Swim for it. Now. I'll be right back."

Even saying the words, I can feel a quivering building up inside me.

"Okay? Magnus?"

I know I have no time to waste. I have to go now. I look out at the water. Goodbye, wreck. My heart spins. I look back up at Pogo.

"You stay here, boy. I'm going to get the boat. I'll be back for you. I promise."

He sets his ears back and hums.

"I mean it. You stay here, Pogo."

I look back at the water. "Magnus," I call, leaning over the hatchway. "I'll be back."

"Sam."

I can't wait any longer. "I'll be right back, Magnus."

"Sam," he calls again.

I know I need to step into the water but fear numbs me. I cannot move. I grip a stanchion, my knuckles so taut they are white and mottled with yellow. The water rises almost to my feet.

Never before have I been unable to make myself do what I know I have to do. My heart churns. I cannot make myself enter the water.

My eyes are rooted to the water rising and falling before me, the tongue of water lapping toward my feet. Whenever I try to step forward, I feel a force lock me in place.

Then I look out at the boat. The sail looks smaller. Is it heading away? The boat is leaving without me. She came back once. She won't come back again. Now's my last chance.

"Sam?" Magnus calls from down below.

I bite back nausea as I release my grip and go into the water. The iron cold closes around my ankles, calves, knees. Then I let myself slide forward, hearing Pogo hum behind me. I push off, leaving a small rippling wake. My breath comes in ragged gasps. My splashes seem deafening. *Don't make so much noise.*

I feel the safety of the wreck dropping away from me.

I don't dare look down. The depth of the water seems to grow below me, the deeps opening, leaving me exposed.

I swim in short strokes, trying to stay as high out of the water as possible, to move over the surface like a water strider.

Now that I am in the water, *Scallop* is eye-level with me. She looks tiny and dainty and distant.

Slow. Slow. Go slow. Go steady. The farther I swim from the wreck, the smaller I feel. *Make me smaller*—smaller and smaller so I can't be seen. So I won't be eaten.

Fear burns through me and I stroke faster, my eyes unmoving from the boat ahead. If it gets me, I'll never see Pogo again.

I keep stroking over the smooth swells. In a trough, I see only the top of the mast and the sail ahead. I rise up the side of a swell to see the boat rocking on another swell, then dipping away into a trough. I'm getting no closer. Maybe the tide's against me.

My breathing comes in rapid pants, my lungs a rasping bellows.

I'm not going to make it. I'm going to sink. I'm going to drown.

I feel my body tense and grow heavy as if it is becoming stone. *Don't go so fast. Don't splash. Just keep swimming.*

The low sun sends the shadow of my head stretching across the water. In the sky above the boat, a lone gannet flaps past. It turns its head to look at me, gliding for a moment, then flaps onward.

Closer. It's closer now.

My legs feel thick and frozen and weak. I think of all the fathoms of ocean below me, the dark water, the unseen creatures.

Rest. Turn over on your back. Just for a second. As I turn I take in a mouthful of water and gag. I cough, my throat burning with salt water, and turn back on my stomach.

The sun angles across the water from behind the wreck. Silhouetted by the low sun, the wreck looks like a rock formation jutting from the sea, just the way it did when I first sighted it. That light spot halfway up the deck must be Pogo.

How far away am I? *Keep going.*

I stroke forward, *Scallop* now so close I hear the rigging rattle and slap as the boat rocks on the slow swells. The sound sends me stroking harder.

A blur passes over me. A black bird circles past—a cormorant.

I keep stroking as the bird circles around me.

The cormorant. The one-eyed cormorant.

I feel a wave of warmth flow through me, and I laugh and gasp and sputter. "You made it," I say to the bird, my voice swallowed by the sea. "You're here."

The bird circles. It carries a fish in its beak.

The boat is closer, and she swings stern-to so that I can read the nameboard, the lettering set between two carved shells: SCALLOP

The boom nods back and forth, the sheet cleated tight. The sail slaps. I see the line that slipped its knot still tied to the bow cleat, dangling over the port bow.

Closer. Almost there. *Don't look down.*

The boat rides low and rocks with a sluggish motion. Must be full of water.

The bird glides in front of me and flares its wings. It stretches out its webbed feet and skis across the water surface to a stop. I slow down to watch it. The bird turns and swims toward me, tipping its beak up to raise the wriggling fish. I want to swim to the bird, but I know I have to keep going. "Sorry," I say. "I'm sorry. I can't wait."

I hear the boat's hull slap the water. The rigging clatters. I look up at the sail and see that the stitches I put in are loosened but still holding. Along the hull stretches a long scrape slashed with black paint from the tugboat's hull. A blotch of rust stain shows near the stern, the work of the barge.

I look back at the cormorant as it nears me. Could I bring the bird with us? Is it bringing me more food?

A shadow deep below my feet freezes me.

I feel myself sinking but I cannot move.

The shadow glides deep enough so that all I see is its black back. It passes out of sight at an angle. It's here.

Scallop is twenty-five feet away—just two boat lengths.

You have to move, I tell myself.

I feel my arms push through the water, my sodden clothes now weighing me down. Seawater spurts into my nose and mouth and I gag and spit it out. I'm not moving. I can't get there.

The bird stops swimming.

I glance back. The cormorant looks around, then looks down into the water. It looks up at me, raises its wings and flaps them.

Then it paddles its feet, heading away from me, the fish writhing in its beak.

Go. Go. Get away. Get out of the water. Fly.

Then I hear a splash behind me, and then a series of rapid, desperate hums, and I twist my head around to see Pogo, at the crest of a swell, battering through the water toward me.

"Pogo!" I shout. "Go back. No, wait. Hurry up! Hurry!"

The bird flaps harder and rises up on the water, running on the surface, leaving a washboard of footprints behind it as it skitters to take off.

I see the shadow pour from under the boat. It hangs beneath me. I fight the urge to try to launch myself out of the water just like the cormorant.

"Don't flail," Steve said.

Then the shadow shoots away, rocketing off as fast as the Coast Guard jet that swooped over my head.

Don't let it be Pogo!

I can see where it's aiming. "No! Look out!"

For a moment I see the bird gain lift, its feet still paddling, its wings beating hard.

Then the water below it bursts and a mountain of black and silver and blue and eyeball white and jagged teeth erupts and then crashes with an explosion of spray and waves.

A swell rolls up where the bird was.

I blink.

The swell rolls on.

I start shaking as I turn back to the boat and thrash and kick. Six, five, four feet away . . . I thrust out my right hand for the rudder and smash my hand on its top.

Got to get it. Got to get Pogo.

I draw my right foot up for a toehold on the rudder, my left leg dangling in the water. Over my shoulder I scream, "Hurry, Pogo! Keep swimming!"

I reach up with my left arm and grab the thin metal bar of the traveler. I pull myself up, grunting, waiting for the crush of rows of teeth to close over my leg. I double over on the transom, drops streaming into the water, my left foot and calf still dangling, still submerged.

I look back behind me to see Pogo floundering in the trough of a swell.

Then I look down. The shadow is coursing toward me.

I jerk my leg out of the water and scramble over the rail and splash into six inches of water in the cockpit. My chest heaving, I lie in the water wheezing, waiting for the shock of the impact.

I tense, picturing the shark rising to erase the bird, rising to ram the boat, to take Pogo.

My anger grows as I picture the shark. Why did it have to do it? Why did it have to kill the bird?

The boat yaws up a swell. Got to get Pogo.

I leap up, unlash the tiller and sheet in the sail. I look back and see Pogo splashing but not making any headway. He's exhausted. He's tipping his snout up to try to stay afloat. The sail hangs limp.

I tear the paddle out from beneath the foredeck and begin chopping at the water, *Scallop* coming around, heading back toward Pogo. A blue-black dorsal fin slashes into view, slices past the boat, then shears through a swell.

Anger like a hot wave crashes through me. "You're not getting my dog!" I scream.

The fin slips below the water.

Pogo is dead ahead, paddling with only his forepaws, trying to keep his head up. The boat slips beside him and I lunge over the rail to grab for him.

I can see the white terror in his eyes as he kicks up foam around him.

I grab his harness and tug, but all I can do is pull him halfway up. I don't have the strength to pull him aboard.

I look back at the sail, and I realize that my only chance is to use the rigging.

"Hang on, Pogo," I say, letting go of him and grabbing the knot at the end of the sheet. I fumble with it, my hands still numb from the water. My thumbs cannot loosen it. Then the knot pops loose and I rip the free line through the block.

Pogo is slipping under and I grab hold of his harness and pull him up. He surfaces with a gasp, his teeth bared, and I thread the free end of the line through the harness and fasten it with two half hitches. "Stay with me," I gasp, and I take hold of the sheet and haul down, the line going through the block and tautening till it hoists Pogo up. I fall back, hauling with my entire body, and he rises with his legs limp.

I reach out to swing him over the rail just as I see the shadow shooting toward us. I clamp on to Pogo and pull him toward me. The water below erupts and the boat tips and we tumble into the cockpit together.

We lie in the sloshing water, both panting. I wait for another thrust from below. I put my hand on his side and stroke his fur. The boat rocks, easing up a swell. I push myself up onto my knees and look overboard just in time to see the shadow arrow away, on a course for the wreck. I watch till the shadow disappears beneath the swells. I sigh. Hating the shark is like hating a tornado. It's a force. A force of nature. It will always be there.

My hands shaking, I splash beneath the foredeck to see if Pogo's canteen is still aboard. I find it in the forepeak.

I unscrew the lid and offer it to him. He stands and shakes off a cascade of water, splashing it into my face. Then he leans his head toward me and takes a few laps.

"There," I say, wiping my eyes with one hand. "That's better."

He pants fast, his eyes still darting with fear.

"Good boy," I say, stroking his back. "You rest. It's okay now. Let me bail so you can lie down."

I put the canteen away and look for the hand pump and the bailer.

The hand pump has vanished, but I spot the bailer beneath a fluke of the anchor.

I bail so hard I don't know if I am gasping or sobbing.

Chapter Twenty-Nine

The sun balances on top of Malabar.

I stop bailing for a moment to watch it bulge and sink behind it. A single cloud shaped like a knife blade above the island turns orange. In moments it turns purple.

I hold the bailer in my quivering hand as I kneel down to lift a floorboard and check the bilge. Only an inch of water remains between the ribs and the centerboard trunk.

I stow the bailer, then reach up onto the foredeck to coil the line so it no longer dangles overboard.

Pogo still lies on his side, panting.

I dig the paddle into the smooth water to bring the bow around. Got to get Magnus. While I bailed, the tide was setting us away from the wreck. I turn the boat around and paddle toward it, the blue of the sky deepening as we move across the water.

I take three strokes to port, three strokes to starboard.

Pogo stays in one spot, not even lifting his head to see what I'm doing, no longer thinking I'm playing some kind of game.

"I'll get you home, boy. Just rest. We'll get Magnus and be on our way."

I think of the direction the shark went in. It must be patrolling the wreck for seals. High above the boat, gulls fly toward the island, the undersides of their wings tinted rose. Why did the cormorant have to die? It saved us. I haven't saved anyone.

The shape of the wreck is becoming indistinct against the darker sea. Are we making any headway? I look up and see a pale moon rising. A star flickers beside it.

My arms are becoming rubbery, my knees hot with pain from kneeling on the wooden deck. *Keep paddling.* Flames begin to tear through my shoulders. My fists scream with cramps. Every time I lean over the side to paddle, I wince when I knock my ribs against the rail. Need to rest. Can't. The tide will set me back.

The whimper that comes out of my mouth surprises me. Am I making that sound? I sound like Pogo. With each stroke I gasp with pain, weakness overtaking me like the darkness growing around us.

I glance down at Pogo. His chest rises and falls, but he's not moving.

A spurt of anger fuels me to take a mighty stroke with the paddle, one so hard I lose my grip. The paddle splashes into the water and slips away behind the boat. I leap up and throw myself onto the transom, reaching over for the paddle. Stretching as far as I can, I can only brush the paddle with my fingertips. It spins away and floats farther off.

Get the boat hook. I spring across the cockpit to reach beneath the foredeck. I feel for the boat hook, grab it and yank. Its hook snags on the coil of anchor line. *Come on. Come on.* I wrench it free and fling myself back to the transom. I twist the aluminum sections to telescope them out but the pole is crusted with corrosion and will not budge. I lean out, holding the boat hook by the tip of its handle. I swipe at the paddle. The hook splashes a foot from it.

Please.

I lean farther over the transom, my left hand gripping the main sheet, and reach out over the water, straining. I lose my balance and let go of the boat hook. It splashes into the water as I slam my hand on the rail to break my fall. I pull myself back up, the image of the shark taking the cormorant flashing before me. I peer across the water. I can't make out the paddle in the twilight. I see the form of the boat hook as it rides up a swell.

I think of the cockpit cover support—the length of varnished wood that acts as a ridgepole for the cover. It is still stowed beneath the foredeck. But even that isn't long enough to reach. I could fashion a lasso with the anchor line.

I kneel down beside Pogo and fold my arms on the rail. I can no longer see the paddle or the boat hook in the gloom. Nothing will work now.

In the west, the last of the light fades silver-blue into the sea. I rest my cheek on my arms and listen to the small splashing of the water against the hull.

Then I let myself lie back on the cockpit floorboards and pull Pogo close to me. I look up at the stars speckling the sky. The boat rides up a low swell. I brush my hand over Pogo, then let it rest on his side. *This is our home now*, I say to myself. *Scallop. Scallop* is our home. The sea is our home.

This is our home forever.

We drift and drift beneath the stars, and I watch them turning until I see a form block them from view, and I wonder why the stars have disappeared.

What's happening now? How long have I been lying here?

Then I feel fingers of air trace coolness across my face. The boom swings back, and the stars reappear. I'll just lie here. I want to stare at the stars. The breeze brushes over me again, and the boom swings around to shake the rigging.

Let me just lie here.

The boom swings again. *Scallop* rocks over a wave. The tiller slaps one way, then the other. The rigging shakes with an impatient chatter.

I grab the rail and pull myself up. A puff of wind greets me. A breeze. A breeze.

I glance at the moon. It rides higher in the sky, its light making a glittering path across the water.

I feel the breeze again. Must be coming from the north.

I take the tiller and pull in the sheet, tightening the sail as I bring the bow of the boat through the wind. Will it last? Will it last long enough before the fog comes back—long enough to go get Magnus?

The breeze fills the sail with a thump and drives the boat across the water, the wavelets clipping against the hull. I feel the energy of the boat vibrate through the tiller. I keep my eye on the moon, now as bright as a spotlight turned toward me. I slack the sheet to let the sail bell out as I shape my course. The boat slips onward, pushed by the steady breeze. Behind us the wake unfurls, streaked with phosphorescence.

I see the shape of Pogo lying on the deck, and I reach a hand out to rest it on his side. I can feel his ribs rise and fall, rise and fall. "Good boy," I whisper. "We're sailing."

The sturdy boat sliding over the low swells, the taut sail and rigging, the firm tiller in my grip, the steady breeze driving us fill my chest with a warm glow as if a lamp has been lit inside me. This is it. The way—the way to save Magnus, the way to get home.

We sail on, and I narrow my eyes to try to make out the shape of the wreck. A glint in the distance catches my eye. A shape appears, and soon the craggy bulk of the wreck is in view.

I tighten the sheet and bring the boat closer to the wind to head for the wreck. The wind holds, pushing us over the low waves. As we draw near the wreck, I hear the wash of the swells pushing in and out of the hull.

I think of the shark swimming inside the ship, and the seal that is no more. I think of our nights in the compartment. We'd be goners if we'd never found the wreck. Then the thought of how I'm going to get Magnus off the wreck and into *Scallop* hits me.

I look up at the towering bow as we sail closer. The rail is lined with the silhouettes of cormorants.

"Hello," I say, my voice echoing against the hulk. "Too bad you can't help me."

I ease the sheet, the sail spilling the breeze, and *Scallop* slows. I aim for the same spot where we first put in.

Chapter Thirty

The sail luffs, rippling loose. I let go of the tiller and hustle onto the foredeck and grab the line.

I glance back at Pogo. "You wait here. I'll be right back."

In the moonlight I see him lift his head for a moment, then drop it back down.

The bow bumps the hull and I stretch out to take hold of the rail, then gather myself, scan the water for a fin, and leap across the gap to crunch onto the slope of the wreck. The crumbling steel plates feel familiar, safe.

The knot I tie around the stanchion can't come undone, I tell myself. But before I head up to the hatchway, I double-check it.

I look back at *Scallop*. "Wait for me," I whisper.

I don't want to scare Magnus, so I don't call out to him as I climb up. I peer over the hatchway lip. The moonlight is so strong it filters through some of the pinholes and cracks in the hull, and lights the compartment. Below, I can see his legs stretched out.

"Magnus," I whisper. "Are you okay?"

I step onto the ladder and start down. "Magnus?" I say louder.

At the last step, I stop. He hasn't moved. I lean forward to peer into the compartment. What if the worst has happened? What if this wreck is where he'll be forever, his tomb, and I am the one to blame for it?

"Magnus?" I shout.

A flutter of wings rises toward me and I see Fuego in the moonlight lift up from Magnus, then drop back down.

"Sam?"

I jump to the slanted floor and rush over to him and kneel down. Fuego flaps his wings.

"Magnus!" I take his hand in mine and squeeze it, and he pushes himself up and claps his other hand on my shoulder.

"That was one long . . ."—he says, his gravelly voice catching—"that was one long swim."

For only the second time in two days, I laugh. "Sorry," I say. "Can you get up? I got the boat. We have to go."

He exhales.

"And Pogo?"

"In the boat. How is the ankle? Is the pain . . ."

"The pain is the pain. We must go. You are right. We cannot delay."

Steve told me after I broke my arm that I should have bound it to protect it as I made my way home instead of carrying it like a sick pet. But I had left my towel behind.

"Magnus, maybe we should wrap your ankle. If you bang it . . ." I point to the rolled-up cover. "That would work."

He nods.

I take out my knife and pry the blade out of its rusted slot. I bend down and ease the cover from beneath his ankle. I hear Magnus suck in his breath.

"Sorry," I say.

Spreading open the cover, I cut out a two- by three-foot strip, then slide it under his leg and ease the material around the ankle, wrapping the length of it from the shin down over his boot. "Tell me if this hurts too much." I take the ends and begin to snug them tight.

He inhales again.

"Sorry. That'll have to do."

I stand up and offer him my hand.

He takes it and I lean back and hoist him up. He looms above me, my head only reaching his shoulders.

"You can put your weight on me. Ready to go up?"

We shuffle and hobble over to the ladder, Fuego on his shoulder. Magnus keeps his hurt leg bent, his foot held above the floor. Each time he hops he leans down, his weight like a tree falling on me.

"I'll have to climb," he says, looking up at the hatchway, "the way I did before. Like an inchworm."

"Okay."

He goes ahead of me. I stay behind him to support him. Every time he gains ground, he groans. I know I can't make him go faster. I picture Pogo standing up, looking around and climbing onto the foredeck, about to try to jump onto the wreck.

The shark will be waiting.

Magnus stops.

"You okay?" I look up at him. The stars surround his silhouette.

"Rest," he says. "Just for a moment."

I want to rush ahead of him so I can check on Pogo. But I hold myself back.

He pushes again, and hoists himself onto the rim of the hatchway. He breathes in the cool sea air. "So good," he says. "So good to be out of the morgue."

I jump past Magnus to check the boat below. Pogo is standing in the cockpit, and I can hear him hum.

"Stay, boy!" I call. "We'll be right there!"

A swell washes against the hull.

I scramble back and help Magnus hitch himself around to a sitting position. Then we start, the slope letting him slide down the deck.

"Don't go too fast," I say, locking my arm around his and pulling back to slow him. If he breaks loose, he'll hurtle right down the deck into the water. He's gaining momentum, his weight pulling away from me. Fuego hops into the air, bouncing between Magnus and me.

"Hold on," I say, planting my feet before me and straining back on his arm.

He sticks out his good foot to break his slide, keeping his hurt one raised. We're both shifting sideways as we slide. He gasps. We're nearing the last stanchions and the water beyond them. Keeping a grip on his forearm, I throw my other arm out and bang it against a stanchion, grip it and haul myself toward it. My hand slips off his forearm and I manage to clamp onto his wrist.

We sweep around to a stop and lie panting just above the water. Fuego lands on Magnus's shoulder.

The boat floats just below us off the rail.

Magnus groans, his chest heaving.

"Can you hold on?" I say. "I have to get another line."

I see him look at the stanchion where I tied his boat. The knot remains. "I had more line aboard," he says. "More line, warm clothing, a first-aid kit, water, food, an outboard, a radio . . ."

"What should we do," I say, "with what's left of her?"

He looks at me, then shakes his head and looks away. "Leave her," he whispers.

Then he turns to me. "Be careful."

I skid down to the level of *Scallop*, haul her by the line toward me, then leap onto the foredeck and step into the cockpit.

Pogo rushes toward me, wriggling in happiness, his tail thrashing his sides. I throw my arms around him and he laps my face.

"Almost there! You're a good, good boy."

I know we have no extra line aboard except for the anchor line, so I yank it out, measure about fifteen feet of it and cut it with my knife.

"Be right back," I tell Pogo. "You stay."

I pull the boat back to the hull, crouch, scan the water, then leap back onto the wreck. I crawl up beside Magnus. "I'm going to tie this around you," I say. "Let's get as close to the boat as we can, and then you put your legs over the side. I'll bring the boat up and you step down onto the foredeck."

He looks down at the boat.

"You mean jump onto the boat," he says, looking back up at me, "on one leg. Well enough. We have no other choice."

"One thing," I say, coiling the line. "Can't fall in. Something's here, a shark—"

"Sam," says Magnus. "Falling overboard is not a choice. Shark or no shark."

I hear Pogo hum.

"Okay."

We creep down to the last stanchion. I reach over for the line and bring *Scallop* up.

"Ready?"

He maneuvers his legs around so they dangle over the hull, his boots about four feet above the foredeck.

I loop the line around his chest, hitch it, then take a turn around the stanchion. A swell rises beneath *Scallop*, shining in the moonlight, and raises the foredeck to within a foot of Magnus.

So much can go wrong. I can miscalculate the swell and let Magnus drop too far. I can let the line slip out of my hands, lose my balance and slide down the deck, fall into the water. He can hit the foredeck too hard and break through it, fall overboard. The shark can come for him. The shark can come for me.

"Okay," I say. "Soon as the boat rises, let yourself down."

I tighten up on the line as he slides down. The line is sliding through my hands, his weight pulling me forward.

Pogo hums.

I hear the water slosh between the wreck and the boat. Fuego flaps, the moonlight white on his wings. I hear a thump and a groan and the line goes slack. I know something will go wrong.

But nothing has. He is on the boat, standing on the foredeck, holding on to the mast.

"Okay," he calls. "I'm aboard."

For the third time, I laugh. "Okay!" I call, unwinding the line. "Right behind you!" I grab the line and slide down to the rail.

"Hang on," I say to Magnus. "I'll help you into the cockpit. Just stay there." I coil the line and toss it over to the boat. It lands on the foredeck. I take a breath. All I have to do is cross the small gap of water to get to my boat, my dog, my friend.

I look back, up to the hatchway and beyond to the bow. Cormorants stand in silhouette in the moonlight. The wreck sways as a swell rolls past. I peer into the water between the wreck and the boat. Don't make a mistake, I think. It's down there, and you know it.

I take hold of the line and draw the boat closer, then wait for a swell. I see one rising toward me, its surface twinkling in the moonlight. "Here goes." I push off, the foredeck coming toward me, and hit the surface with both feet, feeling the boat dip under my weight as I grab hold of Magnus.

"Made it!"

Magnus rests a hand on my shoulder. "Yes," he says. "Yes, we did."

I watch the wreck recede as *Scallop* carries us away, the silhouettes of the birds shrinking and then blending in with the dark upthrust mass of the hull.

Magnus is stretched out beside me on the other side of the tiller, his head on the deck, my sweatshirt his pillow, his foot resting on my duffel. I hear his breathing, rough but steady.

Fuego perches on my shoulder, swaying with the motion of the boat. Then he flaps back to Magnus and nestles down on his chest.

Pogo is lying in front of me, his belly warming my feet.

I turn to look ahead and watch the moonlight-washed horizon. There. In the dusty light I see the low dark line of Malabar. There it is.

The breeze keeps blowing. The moon floats higher as we cross the distance from the wreck.

Pogo raises his snout, then lays his head back down on the deck.

Ahead the island takes on more definition, its dunes pale

in the moonlight. I hear the waves sigh as they run up on the long beach. I adjust our course to stay inshore, in the channel, rounding below Outer Point. I watch the beach appear as we pass on *Scallop*'s best point of sail, a beam reach. I hear the thud and wash of the breakers. Around the sandbar sloping from the point, I tighten the sheet and peer along the beach to where we waved goodbye to Magnus.

I look up at the stars and breathe out in a long stream. I let my eyes slide to the highest point in the sky, and I see it. Among the stars a long, dusty ribbon soars overhead from horizon to horizon. It's the Milky Way, showing me the way.

I know we will be home soon. And Steve will never be home again, forever on the other side of the wall. But I also know he will always be home, back home with me.

Then, in the water by the bow, I see a shape leaving a trail of phosphorescence. I sit up. I clamp on to the tiller, my blood charging into my chest. The shape rises higher—and a fin surfaces.

But it is not the shark's fin.

A dolphin bursts into the air. It hangs suspended for a moment, moonlight silver on its slick back, before diving back down.

"Look!" I whisper. "A dolphin!"

I hear Magnus breathing, breathing, but he does not stir.

Pogo lifts his head. He struggles to get up, his toenails scratching on the deck. I reach out and lift him by his harness.

He points his snout toward the dolphin swimming along-side. The dolphin bounds from the water again, then plunges back in, splashing us.

Pogo shakes. The tips of his ears lift in the breeze as he watches the dolphin angle away.

"Good boy." I rest my hand on his back.

His tail wags, patting my knees. He looks back, a glint of moonlight in his eyes.

And I see him smiling, smiling at me.